LOVE OF NINE TAILED

GUNDRATHI POOJA

ISBN 979-888555156-4

LOVE OF NINE TAILED

Fox red stone of nine tailed fox

About a female collage student love who accidentally swallows the stone of fox, who was achieving his goal of becoming human.

PART 1

Contents

Foreword

PART 1

A myth says when the fox becomes 100 years old, it can become a beautiful women and it can become a men and mate with a women. Once the fox become men it cannot get back to women, it can only turns into a form of men. The fox that lives 1000 years flows through heaven and becomes a heavenly guard. When fox lives with 1000 years then it can become human permanently by losing all powers and then live like human with normal life.

Once a fox completes with 100 years with good virtue just taking energy from human with opposite gender. It can get a fox red stone, if it completes 200 years then it can get 2 fox red stones, as follows for 300year 3 fox red stone, as same as for 900 years it gets fox red stones. At 901 year all 9 fox red stone will converts to a powerful single fox red stone. Finally at 1000 year powerful fox red stone turns in to blue which indicates the fox have turned totally in to human.

A fox complete with 100 years and gets one fox red stone and transforms in to a beautiful women. As he choose to turn in to men. it transfers fox red stone to human with opposite gender to get energy and takes it back when human energy downs to half of normal energy of human by erasing their memories. As same when he complete 200years. finally fox gets 9 fox red stones and it turns to powerful single fox red stone at the age of 901 and he was on the last year which he needs to turn to human that he was at 999 old now...

If you go long enough, you become indifferent to everything. The change of seasons meaning less time that must be spent pretend to be effected love and that emptiness that fills you from time to time, all you feel is the endless repetitiveness.

Fox thinks as when he was in the bar, how much longer must I spend living my life in this absence of compulsion to or toward one thing or another. A girl who is in the same bar comes to him and asks, you seem to be here alone, as always. She just turns around and turns back to him but he will get disappeared without a sign.

He reaches to a library. When he is about to enter library. There come two girls saying "hello writer peter" he smiles to then and enters to library and have a seat. There comes a news in the TV which he was watching "last day, in the middle of the day, in the middle of the city, one women has been murdered brutally. Over 1000 people cross over or pass through that area. Even though there is no evidence found from any CCTV footage and there is no trace of criminal of the mysterious killing of a woman. And there was no witness found and it's making hard to guess culprit's approximately where about, this the biggest hallmark is."

Next day, he wakes up to an alarm, turns it off and he gets ready then, steps out with an umbrella to wedding ceremony hall where bride having ready to get wedding.

After reaching to wedding ceremony entrance, two women get in to conversation. One of them says, "Why it is raining when it wasn't in the forecast?" Other says, "I don't know. I just had my hair done" with irritation. It's all wet, first person says. Then, peter speaks out by looking to rain "it's because it's the day the fox is getting married" both girls look him with confusion. He reaches to bride room and asks her "you didn't send me an invitation. She says with fear, "why are you here brother peter". "After eating so many innocent young people, are you expecting happy ending like his by marring?" "Sorry brother peter I won't do this again please don't kill me." He turns around and says how can you live with so much of sin? You can't be spared. She attacks him but as he was heaven protector he wins to her and kills her. Then all gets disappeared. And there will be no evidence bride.

He goes to library and having a project with other 3 partner girls who are history writers then, one of them says "our theme for this project is the history behind history. I would lie to focus on the behind the stories of our history. Of course there may be difficulty in providing historical evidence, but I think it might be alright if we conduct through research." Then Mr. Peter says "yes, we won't get any problem for this problem as I lived all time since 999 years". All girls look him silently by hearing all there words. And the girl speaks out "wow... Some might hear that and think you really did it yourself. I knew it your works are capable of attracting and holding interest because you write like you have experienced everything yourself." Other girl says "you are right". First girl says "writer peter you are the perfect match to this project". Ok that's all for today. All mentions "thank you". Writer peter writer peter?

Yes, "Writer peter if you have time can we all have lunch now as partners", "no thanks we can have next time, I got to go bye. Then he leaves the place. Girl splits out "that irritates, next time, next time, and next time." She sighs "so when will be the next time"?

On the other side, a boy called jinn had breakup with his girlfriend and shares his sadness to their best friends named with Lilly and Swetha and he drinks too much at that late night. Lilly helps him to him to lift him to his place but he is unable to walk sturdily she tried hard to get him home but suddenly they fell off. Jinn stands up runs firstly forward even Lilly calls him and chase him, while chasing him she says "I will kill you got caught" jinn wait. Too little while jinn fell off on a car and cries by hugging the car "baby don't leave me please". Lilly comes and see this and gets shocked that he spoils car a little with a scratch and she fears the worst and looks around and there she see a person who is standing by starring to stars.

Lilly speaks out, "by any chance, is this your car?" the person will turn to her with wonderful handsome delight face; he is not other than writer peter. Lilly gets stunned by seeing him and says for self "he is human or came from heaven? Then, she comes to consciousness and says him "I'm sorry. I'm sorry" by folding her hands. "Hay jinn, jinn? Wakeup have you gone crazy; get down, hay get down! He falls down from the car. You idiot, get up, let's go. "Jinn crying "I can't go from my love no" he hits the car with legs from laying state. Hay jinn please don't do it, hay please stops, and you can't do this. Please stop. Yes good boy you will stop I know. Peter splits out "you friend must be drunk". "Yes, he drank a little much". "I will give you my number. We will get to pay for..." peter speaks of "are you a student?" "Yes I'm in collage" peter says "then forget it you can go it not damaged badly". When he says this, she says for him "he is an angle" "what?" "what Anhh no nothing, then thank you so much, am sorry" jinn stands suddenly and says "why are sorrying for him? How much do I need to pay him? I will pay him." Then Lilly splits out "we won't have enough even we sold off our organs, so shut your mouth". Ok mister we are sorry jinn say him that you were sorry!" "We are sorry". Jinn please try for walking sturdily ok, jinn nodes head, "ok good boy, and let's go".

Suddenly she touch her leg for herself then, jinn fells of and Lilly about to fall but peter helps her out, in the process of helping unknowing Lilly hits on peter chest then the powerful fox red stone comes out from his mouth and fells on Lilly mouth that she gets swallowed it then it reaches to her stomach. And she gets unconsciousness on her friend.

Later she wakes up from a sofa by saying "my head hurts, when I got home last night? Let's drink some water first" then she opens her eyes and she gets shocked by seeing the house that where she was!

"You are up". "Who are you?" and turns around sees peter and by seeing him she mentions "aren't you the owner of that red car?" "I'm glad you remember it. OH and this... my house." "Why am here" "you didn't wake up, so I had to bring you here. And I have something to get back from you, too." She thinks off and says "something to get back from me?" "You swallowed my fox red stone last night. A very important red stone that I've carried for nearly a 1000 years in order to become a human." She gets confused and says "to become human" what do you mean?" "Oh, I haven't introduced myself yet. I'm a... fox." "[is he mad or what!] I see "says this and moves back to get out of house slowly. He smiles and says "You don't believe me." "No, I do. I believe you, so you are fox, and I swallowed a fox red tone last night. Then watt should I do? Should I go get my stomach cut off at the hospital?" She says this by moving back slowly. "It's not your stomach. It already placed itself in your body." "Then what should we do?" "I have to start looking for a way." "Wait where my phone is? "This means we are in the same situation now. We have shared a goal, to remove that red stone. So let's live together for now." By shocking she says "sorry, wait, you want me to stay in here with you" "I understand that you feel flustered, that we are strangers, and that red stone is precious to me. How can I be reassured unless I have you before me?" "Ankh OMG I can't believe this guy. I was sorry my friend damaged your car and grateful you didn't leave me on the street, so I was going to let you go with it. But what? A fox? Live together? Stop talking nonsense." See? You don't believe me. I guess it will be easier to understand one you see it for yourself." She sees her mobile dialing to police, "try to not escape from here" she looks back to him. Then she gets a very big shock that he turns in a big fox and scares to death then shouts out like a great scare then she gets unconsciousness.

Later again she wakes up from the sofa and mentions "my head hurts, when did I get home last night? What kind of a dream...?" When she opens her eyes totally she looks up with Mr. Peter and gets shocked. "Did you sleep well?

You seemed very shocked earlier. I will bring cup of tea." After saying this he will move to make a tea. She fears the worst. When Mr. Peter turns back by saying "are you ok with low sugar tea." She gets disappeared. She will be getting run off to her house and locks her house door and within a second someone knocks the doors all of a sudden, she gets fear and cries by saying "I think he came after me" by seeing on a photo she says "mom, Aman, what I'm going to do" then, a voice comes from outside "sister open the door." "Anhh? It's Aman! Aman I'm opening the door" she hurries, when she opens the door she goes to hug him by saying Aman and by worrying. Aman says "move out of my way" when he totally enters she locks the door. "Why are you locking the door? When she was relived then Aman says "what's wrong? Anhh... wait. Are you hungry or what? No wonder you were running so fast." "No, I...." "You ran at full speed so you could eat!" "No it's not that...." "You stayed out all night, and couldn't even find time to eat? You are such a sister." And move "follows him by fear all the time as where is goes. If Aman goes to kitchen to make some food she follows him back, when he goes to fridge she follows him there, as he goes to eat she follow him back, and starring him while he was eating then she thinks "what I'm going to do? I think he is really a fox. What I'm going to do now? I would better not to tell Aman, right? If I do, I might put him in danger, too! "Seriously! Why do you keep following me around?" "Well, I can't tell you why, but I'm too scared to be alone." Sister, you frighten me even more. Go and take a seat.

When Aman was sleeping she gets starring him on his side like ghost. When Aman opens his eyes he gets scared and screams "oh! God" he gets relief after that and says "what's wrong with you today?" "Aman! The fact that you are an archer, that you are good at shooting arrows, might all be fate." "What are you talking about?" "I really don't want to tell you, but I can't find any other way. I'm sorry, can you help me." "What is it" "I met a fox who is leaving for a long time." "What?" "He hasn't done anything yet, but might come for me soon. When he does can you shoot him?" she turns around and says "I have seen people shoot flaming arrows in historical drama" when she turns back by saying "can you do that" Aman was having a target on her with arrow an bow "no, not me. The fox." Fox, my foot. Did you catch yourself in the mirror? Get out of my room." "hear me" "three, two!" by slowing her voice down she says " fine" and she gets out from his room and gets to her room after closing her door she stands there and says "god! Who would believe that? But why is that fox men so quite? It's making me more anxious." On the other hand Mr. Peter was staring out through window...

Next morning she catches the bus to get to collage and thinking off "the world is so peaceful, and I actually met a long lived fox? May be it was just a nightmare. The boy who is sitting in front of her thinks "next stop I should get down" he gets up and walks through door as sudden break applied by the driver the person suddenly touches Lilly hand the, he apologies to her "I'm sorry" "its ok" suddenly a wave appears from her stomach and gets with stomach ache "what's this? What happened to me is that menstrual cramps, but it's not like that" the person behind her asks "hay! Are you ok?" "it's nothing" person looks her holding her stomach and he says "driver stop the bus a girl was having with stomach ache she was in urgency" driver stops the bus. "Everybody move, move, fast." Then she gets down. She slowly reaches to collage. Then she goes to her friend Swetha. Swetha spots her and mention "what happened you are so weak" "I have heavy stomach ache, though it was not menstrual cramps, but it hurts 10times more, why I don't know. "Hay then you shouldn't have gone to hospital!" "I came to repost attendance first. Why this does hurts so much? I even have anything special" then she suddenly thinks off about the incident about the single fox red stone. How it got transferred. A person comes to her and holds her hand tightly and says 'hay Lilly why you are so late to collage today what happened" then she fainted with open eyes getting stomach ache more heavily. Swetha calls her to wakeup "Lilly wake up what happened open your eyes. The boy, who holds hand, will carry her head to wake up and she totally gets unconsciousness.

Then Mr. Peter gets a sign of something and suddenly he receives a call from police station.

In a police station a girl was hitting a man and saying "I will kill you". Then, Mr. Peter comes there and speaks out "why don't to get go before we talk?" She smiles by seeing him and leaves the person whom he was hitting and splits out "you're here. Have you been well? It's our first time since we are free from, so it's been 85years? Did you ever wonder how I was doing?" "We have never checked on each other. Why did you call me?" "Erase their memories for me with your magic." "you can do that for yourself" I can't use magic anymore." "Why not?" he looks her with a meaning "you are right, I became human 4years ago." He goes out without saying anything to her. "You can leave me like this I want take you to lunch for helping me. OH right, a fox hunger I satisfied with human energy, not with food" then he stops there and looks at her. "Sadly you can't get my energy as your meal since I'm a human now. So stay in a contact. "We have been friends for 700 years. We can't just leave like this. Then she leaves the place.

They both moves to a restaurant and have a seat then girl speaks out "when I was a fox I haven't gained any weight, but after turning in to a human in gaining weight when I eat some little more. I'm using antioxidants to maintain my appearance." "If you have lived this long, you should've learned by now. But you still cross the line, like always." "What? A line? What line did I cross?" by smiling "I don't mean that there's an actual line. "It's an idiom that human often use." "Oh, really? But you know what? I became human before such a smart guy like you. How have you not become human yet? And you look like you gave up on gathering human energy some time ago, too. I hope you aren't still being too careful about choosing? The way you used to be." Then they recall the past conversation.

[Mr. Peter sakes her "you again?" she also repeats the same "you again?" Mr. Peter speaks out "once you fall for her, you lose everything, including your liver, then meet you demise after all of your energy I drained. These rumors are all over the capital city." "Rumors are unavoidable when you're this beautiful." "You don't have to drain them to the close to death every time." "Mind your own business. You're so obvious about displeasure. What will you do if the woman refuses you? Humans are such sensitive creatures." "Then I can just hunt other prey. When my heart isn't moved, whichever one I take will only disgust me."]

Girl speaks out "So what you are planning? What are you waiting for? "He answers nothing. "Say something. I'm 200 years younger than you, and I managed to turn into human first. Don't you have any questions about that? Like, how I became human, if I changed sleeping or eating, how the blue the red stone was, whether it was a dark blue, or a gradient! You should beg me to tell you, on your knees." "You are so noisy" girl cool down by the word and mentions "noisy? Fine." "Why don't we get going? I'm expecting a visitor soon." "A visitor? Who?" he answers to no question and leaves that place.

He gets down from the car and moving to house then he spots Lilly coming by looking here and there. Then Lilly finds him they both reach to Mr. Peter garden when they are walking Lilly splits out "so..." then he looks back to see her. Lilly speaks out "I am sick because of that fox red stone, right?" "To be exactly, it's because you touched a man born in the tiger zodiac sign" "a man born in the tiger zodiac sign?" "Tigers prey on foxes, so we are attacked to their energy. And it's worse for me, who born in a cursed and became the only male fox." Then she recalls the incident on the bus that has been touched her hand "men born in the tiger zodiac sign are full of energy, so they are my worst enemies. And you can't even eat chicken because they are allergic to fox." And since you have my red stone, you feel pain when you meet them." "Does that mean I'll be sick? Until the red stone is removed?"

Then he comes near to her and touches her with a gentle manner. "What are you do...?" "Only my touch can remove the pain" "that's ridiculous" after he removes his hand from touching he sees a thing that, red stone changes to blue for a while. "That's why I asked you to stay with me. I thought you might need me too.' She will think of it and she gets all things packed. Her brother will question her. "Why you are going to your friend house." "I have to complete my team assignment we can't do if are far away." "Ok, then did you this mother?" "You know about our family logo, right? Handle your life on your own." "Okay, than be careful" she was afraid and says "Aman if anything happens to me makes a call to police, ok?" "What? Why?" "No, it's nothing, imp leaving bye, bye." "Ok, Bye."

She reaches Mr. Peter home, and stands out by looking around. Mr. Peter was washing his hand because of blood on his hand silently. When Lilly about to enter house, a cat comes in front of her all of sudden, then she fears the worst and says "oh god, you startled me" then she enters the gate walking to the door, while going near the door she once looks to the side of window and fears the worst where Mr. peter was peeping to her through the window. When she turns her head[S1] towards way of the door there Mr. Peter was spotted. "You were just in there. How can you be out here?" "I teleported." "But why would you suddenly...?" "I thought I would help you with the heavy luggage." The he takes her luggage and goes inside then she follows him.

They both enter the house and Mr. Peter says "you can stay in that room." "Ok, thank you." When she supposed to go her hand bag will get down, and all the things will get out from the bag, and she took a knife with her to her safety it got spotted by Mr. Peter and looks at her by picking it up. By a small smile she says "Anhh that's gif for you, you can have it hehe" "knife was a gift" says by nodding head. "Anhh, my mom said, when we go anyone house we should not go empty handed, so I bought this for you can have it." "Gift, ok" "ok I will get going, good night." "Wait, how should I address you?" "As your wish." "Ok, shall I call you, Miss Lilly?" "Okay, I will get going." Then she enters her room.

Having bed, by crying she thinks of "knife have been taken, stay strong." She closes her eyes. Then she hear a sound and says "what's that noise?" then she step down from the bed and looks at the window, she spots Mr. Peter with sharp cutter. He slowly turns back to her, then she gets scared and screams then runs out of the room to hall she suddenly looks the blood flowing on the floor which is coming out from the fridge, she gets scared worst and turns back, then there comes Mr. peter and he steps forward to her, and she steps back then slips to the ground. "Are you ok, Miss Lilly?" she gets scared by staring at sharp cutter. "Oh, this. I trimmed the trees in the garden." "Trimmed the trees?" "Yes, it was time to prune them." "but why would you do that in the middle of the night?" foxes are nocturnal animals" then he looks to the side where blood is flowing on the floor. He looks to that and goes there then opens the fridge and he takes out a pack." "It's goat blood." "What? Goat blood?" "It's one of my favorite foods. The restaurant didn't package it properly. I got blood on my hands earlier, too, and had a hard time washing it off. But, Miss Lilly, you seem to get scared easily. From now on, I'll finish it off while it's fresh, so I don't scare you." He smiles like scary while saying it. "There's so much blood." She gets starring him like that, and she goes to bed again. "I suddenly had to move in with a fox who have powers. I'm scared and anxious. Will I ever get a peaceful night's sleep in this house?"

Next morning, when she was in sleep "aren't you going to college, Miss Lilly? Miss Lilly?" "I'm not nocturnal like you. Who goes to collage at night..." and she open her eyes a little and then opens suspiciously "what? When did I fall asleep?" she comes out from the room. Ehen she looks at the side of kitchen she spots Mr. Peter preparing something. she stares him that he looks like shining star, then she gets to conscious from that and mentions to herself "what are you doing, Lilly get a hold yourself, that man is a fox who tricks human. He is just a sly fox wearing the mask of a shining appearance." Then Mr. Peter looks at her and asks "did you sleep well?" "Yes, I guess." "You don't seem like you did, though. Come have some walnuts. Walnuts protect your liver and help with fatigue." "What? Why does he care about my liver? What does he want to do with it? That sly fox." "Oh, yeah, I don't know what you like yet, so I bought some random things." He opens the fridge and shows it to her. After seeing that she laughs and says. "That sly fox." "I got some ice cream, too." Laughs again. "That sly fox." "And I will take care of your tuition." She forgets to say it to herself and splits out that "generous fox." "What?" "Why would you? You don't need to do that." "I feel bad since you will be burdened with many inconveniences. Since you're a student, I thought paying your tuition could help to make up for it." It's ok, though. Should I text you my banking info? He nodes his head. [Deposit details: Rs. 10, 00,000]. She gets shocked and joy, "this covers both, my tuition for next semester and Aman training!" she was so... excited and happy laughs for herself loudly. Suddenly she looks to the mirror "are you happy? How could you laugh in this situation?" "Miss Lilly." "Yes? Do you want to talk to me?" she comes out of the room and sees that Mr. peter ready with luggage. "Are you going somewhere?" "I'm attending a book event. I wrote books on the humanities." "I see, so you have a job. Even beasts of legend cannot escape capitalism." "It's more that living a long life becomes tired some." "Oh." "Anyway, I'm going to Singapore, and will be away for a few days." "Okay. Really?" "You look so happy. I must've made you very uncomfortable." "No, I wasn't. I'm not happy at all." "Then I'll be going." Then he suddenly changes his form in to an old man. She gets scared and screams out. "What are you doing?" "Its shape shifting. I heard reporters may come, but I don't want to become publicly known. So until I meet with the publishing company staff, I thought I would travel like this." "I see. You are so multitalented." "Okay, then. I'm really leaving. Make sure to lock the door." "Okay."

[In collage.]

All right. "Let's stop here. Please submit your assignments by next week." "Thank you, sir." "Thank you." Swetha calls Lilly "hay, Lilly! Why do you look so down? Are you still sick?" "No, I'm fine now." "That's great. Then you're going to join with us to the party right?" "Party?" "Remember, we're having a farewell party for bobby because she's leaving to go study abroad." "Oh, right. I've been so busy these days that I forgot. But I can't really be in the crowded places right now. We're no longer freshman, living like there's no tomorrow. We need to start worrying about tomorrow's hangover and the coming of old age!" "You're kidding. And you're still young, lacking experience; immature. Just go no matter what you should come that's it." They all will force her. "Fine, fine! Are we going now?"

"No but you should look modern ok, bye see you at evening." Lilly nodes her head.

"Oh... you looks amazing Lilly." "Then what you are looking at lets go" " yes, let's go" they enters he club there a person holds Lilly she mentions "are you interested in going to police station along with me." "Sorry just for fun, bye." Then her mobile fall off from her hand in the crowed place a person will pick it up and acts like giving it. He holds her on her shoulder, then she suddenly come up with heavy stomach ache, Mr. Peter senses something and called her but she won't lift the call "hay miss what happened are you drunk more. Do you want to give a way to your home?" "Please." "Ok, be patience, shall I take you to near where I know." "Please." There corms Mr. peter and takes her from other person hands. Mr. Peter says "I have been looking for you." She gets unconscious on Mr. Peter. "Who are you?" "I'm her friend. I'll take her with me." Peter takes handbag of Lilly and about to move then. "How can I just believe that you're her friend?" peter looks at him with attitude and takes his mobile and makes call to Miss Lilly mobile. It rings another person pocket, he picks it out. "Why do you have my friend's phone?" "Because she's my friend" "do you know her name?" to that question he stands silent. Then peter takes her mobile from his hand hardly. And moves from there. The person comes back of him and holds Mr. Peter to stop him and says "hay." Mr. Peter just kicks with a hand little small force but person goes to a far distance and fall off.

Mr. Peter takes her to a restaurant the takes a seat while she was just unconscious. Then slowly she comes in to conscious but pretends that she hasn't waked up. Mr. Peter identifies her pretenders. "Are you feeling better?" "Miss Lilly do you want to eat ice cream, I'm going to have its, my favorite thing here, its tastes awesome." "Yes, I want ice-cream for 10 more times" she excitedly says this along with pretend. Mr. Peter smiles for her innocence and childishness. She mistakenly says it and again talks for herself "I've actually not drunk up a while ago, but I missed the right time to get up." She silently moves up and starts eating like a moving train very firstly. "I would prefer you scold me... I went club although I knew crowded places are dangerous and made you come back after travelling abroad for work. I'm sorry for everything." "It's ok. The red is fine, so you are fine. But you should avoid places like that from now on; it is only for your sake." "Okay. From now on..." "Don't be scared, either." "What?" I know you're scared of me. You're worried I might harm or threaten you. I can see it." "Well..." "I understand. Who wouldn't scare of fox men? But you're not just anyone. You have my red stone, and you need to be safe to keep my red stone safe. I can only protect you at all costs. So why don't you try to be less scared? It makes me feel bad to see you living on pins and needles." "I'm sorry that I've worried you. From now on, I'll try not to be scared of you, and to keep something like this from happening again." "Do you promise?" "Yes." Then he asks her to promise by having hand in hand, she makes that. When she is about to take her hand of he drags her hand and says "you have to keep your promise." "I will." And then they leaves the place to go home. When they are walking towards the home. "By the way, is the red stone visible only to you?" "Yes." "Do you know how it can take it out?" "I will try; a human cannot carry the stone for long anyway." "How long can a human hold it then?" "Probably, a year." 'So that after one year of carrying it, it will be resolved one way or the other." Then he looks at her. "Doesn't it? Then what happens if it's not taken out in time?" "You will die." "What?" "Miss Lilly, you will die. Then she gets shocked and stands still at one place by starring him...

He grabs her hand and teleports to home with her "you don't have to worry. I just wanted to share the worst that could happen. We still have a year of time, so I'll try to find a way. You should get some rest. Good night." "Look how relaxed he is about this. Is it because it's not his life? Anyway, why didn't he say he was going to teleport? So surprising.

Mr. Peter doing some work on his laptop and his drink gets completed then he is about to bring it so, started to move way to the kitchen. Then he gets scared when he suddenly looks at window. "Whoa". There Miss Lilly stand like ghosted appearance. Then he slowly goes to the window and opens the window. "What are you doing out there?" "I got depressed, so I came out to get some air." "Oh, I see." "You must be busy trying to meet your deadline, Mr. Fox man. There's a deadline on your manuscript and on my life." "Miss Lilly..." she suddenly gets angry and shouts like, "I didn't even hit you that hard. How could it pop right out? Don't you have any muscles? Do you ever work out?" then she leaves the place. When Mr. Peter moves to kitchen, all the stuff was cut off on the table and slowly miss. Lilly stands up from under the table, catching the knife like which look like cutting of people's heads from body. He gets scared by seeing sharp knife on her hand, "Miss Lilly, what are you doing down there?" "This berry fell." "Why are you suddenly...?" "I got hungry after taking a walk. You're probably wondering why I would want a snack now, but I may have less than 365 days to enjoy late-night snakes. I'm going to start have my life to leave no regrets. So. Have you thought about, how you can take the stone out?" "Oh, that..." then she gets anger and by cutting the stuff with rhythm of saying "I hope! You think! Of something! Very soon!" then she after saying the words she starts cutting the onion like cutting a piece of meat nonstop, at that time she looks like crazy person.

She goes to restaurant with jinn and starts her original character action on eating, when she is eating thinks off "I have only 365days, so without regrets I should eat all the foods, I need to live with all my dreams full filling. She eats more food and drinks a lot.

"Jinn I'm going to die. Please give me 100 times of food to my soul after I die." "You are a very crazy girl, you won't die. Let's go." "You idiot you won't believe me get lost." She kicks him. After he went off she is about to walk home while hitting her chest lightly "oh I feel sick, did I drink more?" suddenly she gets her leg kicked for herself and fell down when she open he eyes she looks a red stone which is shining. And says "oh, stone! The stone popped out!" then she was very happy and laughs cunningly. Mr. Peter waits about her in home. Then she runs to him "Mr. Fox! Hay, Mr. Fox! Mr. Fox!" by seeing him she says "hay, Mr. Fox! This is awesome!" then he stands up "I fell down after hitting my chest a few times, then the stone popped out from the impact." "What?" and she very happily shows the stone which she bought with her. "Look. I'm not going to die anymore." Then he looks at her surprisingly and says, "this is... this isn't the stone. I think it's a candy someone spat out." "What?" then she looks at it and which having much dust on the candy. The thing happened in past was that when shell off she looks a candy with shining because a light fells on candy so, it looks like stone with seining. "Darn it. I thought I had saved myself." She gets disappointed, as it was not a stone. "Hay miss lily. At this hour, it's very dangerous for you to walk around in this drunken state..." then she want to throw out all of a sudden. "Are you alright, miss lily" then she looks to pot. Then Mr. Peter thinks, "What is she looking at?" then he looks to it. "That the pot made by the master who made one of the national treasures." He gets worried. Then she throw him from catching her and run towards the pot. Then, Mr. Peter use magic and make the pot to flow. "What? Where did they go? What's going on?" she takes out her hand bag and throws it randomly, it is about to fell on other pot. He again makes the pot to flow in air. She finds other pot. He again use his magic to float then, it will happen repeatedly to all the pots, she behaves like a child, and finally she goes near to the restroom, he will use magic to open the door. She will move to rest room. Then at last he looks to all the pots floating in air. "I can't believe I'm using powers for this." He gets relief all of a sudden a pot fell down and broken down. Mr. Peter gets scared for that "Anhh that was scaring." Later he prepares lemon juice for her hangover and call her "Miss Lilly, Miss Lilly?" she won't answer for him. Then he goes back to his bed.

At morning she stand on kitchen table, takes a pan along with spoon and sounds. "Yah... I'm not scared. Come on!" then makes a sound with pan and spoon! Then shouts like anything. There Mr. Peter get scared and moves to kitchen with hurry "ya... Ya... tad... tad..." "Miss Lilly what happen why are you doing this." "Do you know... balloon, balloon... deal with birds. Stair? Where did the stair come from?" again she makes sound from pan and spoon. "May be it's... sent to help me. Hahaha" she laughs like a fool and makes a sound and totally behaves like child. She comes down from the table. Moves near to Mr. Peter and says "you know the new era of princess should not be weak" she laughs again and makes sounds "so I'm not scared" then she drags his shirt and act kick him on his chest "whoa..." "Are you hurt? Hahaha, bye bye..." then she goes to her room.

She gets ready for collage, and goes to Mr. Peter "Mr. Fox man I'm going to college, Bye." Then she move from him with dancing. "Mr. Peter gets surprised and smile at her behavior.

At collage Lilly, Swetha and jinn walks a while, Swetha asks Lilly "hay, Lilly, what happened at the club? Why you went from there without informing us?" "Oh, something suddenly came up." Jinn says "you left without a word?" "Yes?" "My phone died, so I couldn't contact you. Sorry. Did I keep you guys from partying?" "That's not the case. We had lots of fun partying. I never get bored if I got some beats." There comes a car with higher speed which is about to hit three of them but suddenly its direction have changed and they all safe. Then Lilly speaks out "why the heck drivers like that? Then jinn starts split out "I think that's Sameer." Then Swetha says "what? Guy Sameer? From the batch of 2017? "Yes, the legend of the history department who fooled over 20 women, Sameer. We are doing group project together, so I know him." Swetha smiles and says, "He returned to collage. He was so cool." Lilly says "let's go." Then they all leave the place.

Later Lilly was going back to lunch, so on the way she thinks, "Okay. In order to survive, I have to keep the stone safe." From back Sameer comes there and calls her, "excuse me." Then she turns back and thinks, "Isn't he Sameer? I think he was born in tiger zodiac sign! Jinn said the same thing." "You dropped this." By showing her scarf which is on the floor. "I'm sorry, but could you just leave it on the floor?" "What?" "Just leave it on the floor." Then he drops it and she takes it by avoiding him. "Thank you" she lefts the place. "What's with her? And he also moves from there.

Mr. Peter goes to the girl who met before in the police station. Then goes conversation. "What living together, I get that the stone just rolled in to that women, but how did you of all people decide to live with a human women?" "Well, at first, I thought it seemed interesting, so I wanted to keep her by my side, and..." "And? What?" "Forget it." "Why won't you finish your story? Anyway, does she know that she can die if the stone keeps taking energy?" "I'm not going to let her die." "Okay. I'm glad you made that decision. I hope you won't have to take the stone from her dead body like back then. Anyway, there's something I would like to ask."

When miss lily on way to her home, she met Sameer. she avoids him and moves forward then suddenly a Person come up with bicycle and then she almost to fell off, when Sameer goes to help her from fall of she refuse to get help from him and she gets fell off intentionally without touching him. "Are you okay?" he was about to lift het but she scroll on the floor and run from the place by avoiding him. "Did she just roll over trying to avoid touching me?" the she reaches home.

"What happened Miss Lilly?" "You are asking me what happened, I fell over trying to avoid a guy born in tiger zodiac sign." Then she holds his hand says "Mr. Fox man, I'm so hungry please give me dinner my stomach was empty it making sounds." Then he smiles and they both goes to kitchen. "Miss Lilly I don't know cooking much but I will do it for you by seeing in to YouTube, can you wait for a while?" "Yes," then he smiles and starts working. She goes to get shower and comes back. There Mr. Peter have prepared all food and served her. "What you made Mr. Fox" "since you can't eat chicken so I bought goat meat and prepared it. Wait. Can you eat goat meat?" "No, I can't. I can't have enough of it!" she says very happily, thanks for the food." He laughs for her childishness. "It looks tasty." When she takes one bite "seriously? The flavor, taste, texture are all horrible." "How does it taste? Do you like it?" "Yes. It's tasty. It tastes really good." "I made a lot of it. You can have it all." He was about to serve. "No, wait!" then he gets disappointed and keeps the vessel down. "It's not tasty, right?" "Well... I'm sorry. I appreciate your kindness though." She keeps her hand on stomach that she was hungry, but she acts like she was ok, but peter observes her and says, "I'll go get something to eat." "Don't. I'm okay." "I don't want you to starve because of me. I'll be right back." "But, I'm really okay." He left the house to get some food. "Maybe I should have tried to eat it. It would have made me more patient."

She washes all the vessels and cleans everything. Tens speaks herself "I'll tell him we're having only delivery foods from now on." Then suddenly her stomachs get upset, because of eating food just now, and she was hurry to restroom. She comes out, again it gets upset. She calls to Mr. Peter "hay, Miss Lilly." "How long until you're home?" "I'm almost there." "Already? She worries that he comes fast. "Right. I bought some pizza. Is that okay with you?" "No, it's not. I think greasy food like that can cause trouble and disease like obesity and esophagitis." "I should have asked you before buying it then. Is there anything else you want to eat?" then thinks off "what's the food he can't get near here? Something that takes a long time to get." "Noodles." "Noodles? I'll see if I can find it. Okay." "Now noodles earned me some time, lets recover from this very fast." She takes dill seeds to recover it and she gets relief. And says "now, the pressure is off, both my mind and stomach. Especially my stomach. It feels like my stomach is totally empty." Then she gets worried hard "oh, no." she runs out where she can see Mr. Peter and says by moving towards him, "oh, I have a problem. I think the stone came out. Could you see if the stone is still there?" she shows her stomach to like a child to see whether the stone is in there or not. "The stone is fine." "Really? Ah! Thank goodness." "Did something happen?" "It's just that I had a serious stomach upset and relived for 5 times, I felt like all my organs came out. I was worried that the stone also..." then, he laughs for her words and childishness. Then she stops her words like. "But its fine. Anyway, I'm glad the stone is fine." Then they both enters the house.

They will sit at dining table, pizza and noodles were opened. Then slowly Lilly speaks out by seeing on to pizza, "hay. Can I have a slice of pizza?" "Are you sure? What about esophagitis and gastritis?" "Actually, I gave it some thought, you see, cars need oil to move. I think humans need some oil too to move. I love fat." She shay it with much childishness. He laughs and says "sure. Help yourself." "Thank you" she eats very fast like it gets thrown out. With having a bite, "it's so tasty." "I have a question." "For me? What is it?" "Losing the stone would be a good thing for you." "Right. That's what I want." "Then why were you so relieved when I said the stone was still there?" "I do wish the stone is gone, but I wish it happens safely. I don't want the stone to go to the waste. I don't only care about my own life. I care about the stone and your dream, too. What did you think of me, I'm not that selfish?" He feels some happy. "Why don't you have some too?" "I can't satisfy my hunger with human food. Human food is like some sort of snack I eat for pleasure from time to time... and mainly I eat ice-cream every time, it tastes deliberately." "Then why did you cock earlier?" "Because you are hungry" "then did you get these...?" "I got them for you." "Oh, I see."

Later at mid night she wakes up and she finds a light coming from underground and she scared and went to the place to see it. She open the door and get locked she gets scared and tries to open it. She seen Mr. Peter there are gets scared. "Mr. fox" "what are you doing here, Miss Lilly?" "I'm sorry. I'll leave now." He moves towards her. "Please let me get out of here." "I can't." "Why not" "because I'm locked here, too." "What?" 'The doorknob broke, so I was trying to fix it with the drill. I even put the wooden block there to stop the door from shutting." "Why did it fall out then... did I by any chance...kick it when I come inside?" "Yes." "I'm sorry. It's all my fault." "Did you think I locked you up on purpose?" "What? No, no way." Then she laughs. She stops he looks at her. He gives a smile for that." "By the way, how do we get out of here?" "I guess there's only one way." He shows his hand to give something. "right." Then she holds his hand. "What are you doing?" "What?" "I was going to ask you if I could use your phone. To call a carpenter." "I thought you were going to teleport us." "We can't teleport here." "Why not? You did it just fine a few days ago." "Teleporting causes a wave, which can affect the things around you. And I have many important things here." "Oh, I see." "Then he shows his hand, to give her phone. She gives to him, then he makes a call to carpenter. Then, lights were also gets off. 'There must be something over there to light up this place. Wait here." He turns around and thinks for few seconds and turn back again and says, "Hold my hand." "I'm good.' "Okay." When he was about to go she holds his hand and they both moves to inner area. He lights up a lamp then she speaks up, "is this a kerosene lamp?" he uses his magic to light up all the candles in there, they give more lighten to the area. Lilly gets wondered for that place and was very happy. "Wow... what are all these?" "Things that were naturally collected over time." "My god." She gets wondered for that, "This is a bronze dagger, right? OMG you have all dynasties things. "What this." "Once I worked for the science department." "Whoa, you were a scientist? You were such an elite. And what else have you done? I was worked for the back of truth." "You were in the military too. That's why there are swords and bows. Whoa." "Miss Lilly, you seem to be very interested in history, unlike most young people." "Haven't told you yet? I major in history. Some kids applied for this major because of their grades, but in my case, it's because I love history. I want to be a museum custodian after graduation. But I'm sure if I can live until then. Anyway, this is really cool. How does it feel to live a long life?" then he feels disappointed and says, "Nothing. It doesn't feel like anything." She feels bad for it and she diverts it. "Oh, there's a pipe too. Have you used it yourself?" "Yes." "Since when?" "Since tobacco was imported in 1592." "1592? Have been smoking cigarettes for over 400 years then?" Then goes near to him she touches to his liver position and asks "did nothing happen to your liver? Wow... that's great. Then how old are you? I'm 22. Born in year 1999, zodiac of rabbit." "I'm 999. Born in 1012. Relax." "I mean... now that I hear your actual age, I realize how ancient you are. Then you are like fossil man Hahaha." She stops it and says "oh, it's a wind chime. It's so pretty." "You can have it if you like it." "Are you sure? It looks at least a few 100 years old." Then she gives a cute smile. There comes a voice from outside. "Hello?"

They take a walk out for some time, Lilly speaks out "right. Can we talk about how we address each other? I don't feel comfortable calling you Mr. Fox man all the time." "Since I call you by your name, you can call my name too." "No, I can't do that. Your 977 years older than me. It's like I can't call the king of a country by his name. I think it's disrespectful. How about Mr. Landlord? Well, maybe it sounds like you would push me to pay rent. How about Mr. Ancestor? Well, I guess it sounds like you would take food from an ancestral rite. How about sir? How about oldex? It's short for old fox." "Sir, sounds good to me." "It's sir then. Let's get inside, sir." He laughs and says, "Sir..."

When she was studying, she looks at chain which was given by Mr. Peter "he's sweeter and more caring than I thought. And..." she recalls the words. "How does it feel to live a long life? "Nothing. It doesn't feel like anything."

"He looks a bit lonely too." She comes out, then she spots Mr. Peter and moves to him "sir." "Why haven't you gone to bed yet?" "Well, I was doing my assignment and I got sleepy, so I came out to get some fresh air." Then, she feels sad by seeing his face and says, "It's hard, right? You seem tires, so I was worried. Until now, I have been thinking only about my situation, but earlier when I visited the tunnel, I realized how long you have been living. For such a long time, you had one dream. And it can all go down the drain, so I can only imagine how hard it must be. I feel a bit bad too, because it feels like it's my fault." "Why would you feel bad?" "Just because. You know what? How about we try to live through this day? If we repeat that, I believe good days will come in the end. Let's fight it out together. I'll go inside now. Don't think too much." When she going inside he thinks of a question who asked by the girl who became a human earlier. "Anyway, there's something I would like to ask. Do you want to become a human? To be honest, after what happened, I thought you gave up hope. Who is she to turn you like this? You already know how to take the stone out." He turns back and calls her. "Miss lily." "Yes?" he goes to her "let me check one thing." He holds her hand and looks in to stone it's showing red color and says "you can go back now. Just think all this was a dream." then, he is about to hug her to take the stone but suddenly he senses something that stone gets somehow blue. "I will get going." When she was going he feels some sad and drags her hand and hugs her.

She moves to her friends to a café and starts speaking "a person hugged." Swetha says, "He hugged you? "Well, this isn't about me. She's a friend of mine. The guy she lives with... said, "Let me check one thing." "Suddenly wanted to check something, then grabbed her hand. And then he suddenly hugged her. What kind of trick is he playing?" then Swetha speaks out, "what do you mean, a trick? This is why I don't associate with kids who haven't loves before. That's called experiencing affection. What do you think he was trying to check? It's obviously her love. Anyway, you frond got married young." 'Oh, she's not married. She's living with him. But it's not affection. They don't like each other." Then jinn gets shocked and splits out, "what? They live together even though they don't like each other? Why?" "Well, one thing led to another and now she's bearing a precious..." suddenly Swetha wonders and says, "what? She's pregnant?" "She's not pregnant, but... isn't it frustrating? I..."

"You have no idea how to color the rest of the blue." A female fox says this to Mr. Peter. "All I can do for now is keep an eye on her." "I finally get it. You wouldn't let a random human stay by your side. The stone rolled in to her, as if she's the owner right before your thousand years are up. On top of that, although it was only a brief moment it even turned blue. I can see why you thought this was fate. Anyway, be good to her as much as you can." "Why should I do that?" "This might be the last chance you have, and so everything you can as best you can." "Okay."

Next morning he was in bed and opens his eyes he sees that Lilly was checking his heartbeat. "My chest isn't a public dorm." "Sir, I know where that strange heartbeat sound comes from." Then she smiles like a fool. Where Mr. Peter moves her hair back, then she points out his heart position and says, "It seems that if we are far apart, it will continue to beat anxiously." Then he push her forehead with pointed finger. "That's the thing, when you gets hurts I will be knowing. If your mood changes drastically, I can still feel it no matter how far away we are." She was so excited. "Could this be the telepathy that only exists in movies?" "I'd rather call this a mutually retraining effect."

There come Sameer having get-together with his frons in collage. One of his friend says. "guys do you know a girl called Lilly, she is avoiding Sameer even he wants to help him she just rolled on the floor and left, it was hilarious." they all gets laugh" then Sameer says, "she builds a wall against all men, just like that." She even down jinn too." "You're actually comparing me to jinn?" "Fine, you do look much better. But, you both have same impression to her Hahaha." Other person from group says, "Lilly might be the type who's into people's character, not looks." Other says, "Right. I think even Sameer can't get Lilly." Then, Sameer looks to him, "what with that face? Do you feel confident? Let's make a bet and see if she falls for you, then." Other says "that's a very good idea. Let's make a bet for 1lakh. Are you in?" Sameer speaks out, "I'm in." then he follows her in collage like. Gives her cocks, sitting by her side in class. "Is this seat available? Can I share your book?" Then she gives her book to him. When she was studying in library she gets a message from Sameer. "We're all meeting up at the back gate today. Want to come?" "Why does he do this to me?" she will ignore his message. And getting ready to go home, when she was about walk out there comes Sameer in front of her "do you enjoy ghosting people?" "Sorry." "I said were meeting at the back gate." "Right, I have to go home early..." "Then forget today. Let's watch a movie this weekend." "Why do you want to go with me?" "You are coming that's it, bye." "Hay, I don't... why he don't listen me. God."

When she was near to home, Mr. Peter comes there after some walk and he meets her. "Hay, sir, where were you from?" "I had some walk out." "Oh, okay." She suddenly throws her bag inside home and jumps in front of him. Excitedly she asks him that "sir, do you have power to fly!!" "yes." She so surprisingly says, "whoa... really! My lovely boy umha." He gets shocked for her word, she takes him to garden, "quick! Come, come, come! "After they goes to garden, she shows her hands like to catch her, with excitingly. "Come, let's play flying once!" "No. the circumstances were special." She gets disappointed and asks him like a child with crying face by holding his shirt. "Please, please... just one last time. Really just one last time. Just for a little while." She is going on dragging his shirt with cute face. Then he smiles for innocence and cuteness. "You said it's the last time" Then she was very happy and shows her hands to catch her. He holds her in his arms. Then she shows a place at high and says, "I want to go there! Let's go, Pokémon!" they he flies off along with her in arms, she was so excited and very happy by seeing all the things. She looks to him. When they are flying and he too looks at her. There comes a small feel between then for few seconds, and they suddenly gets in to conscious, he lands on the roof top of building. There they spend some time by playing.

There comes weekend he was forcing her to go watch movie with Sameer, then she decides to take Mr. peter help, that she wants to get rid of him, then she was coming home, there food delivery boys are going out from home. She gets suspicious and runs inside home. There she looks all food items opened. "What's all this?" "I thought you might be hungry, so I got these for you." "You got this much food? You don't know what I'd like, so you got everything?" you seemed to like everything, so I got everything. Right, but no chicken." "Whoa... you're such a delicate and considerate guy. Sir, I knew it. I knew you'd be like that, but you seem to be a bigger player than I though." Then she takes her seat to eat. "Sir, you have loved lots of women, right? I mean, you're pretty old. I need the help of someone who's experienced like you. Could you please help me out?" "Can you speaks out about what?" "Here's the thing." Then she explains everything what happened with Sameer. She sighs after saying all those and gets tired, "so in short, you want to disappoint that guy and make sure he never approaches you again?" yes, that's it." "How can I help you?" "Let's go on a date with me." Mr. Peter gets shocked. "A date? "Yes. Just as how we take mock test, I want to go on a stimulation date before I go out with him. I'll do my best to be awful, so tell me what you hated the most, and if you have any ideas on what I can do to get him to hate me more." "Miss Lilly... I know it's you, but I can't intervene with personal..." then she innocently says, "He was born in the tiger zodiac sign." Then he suddenly takes a word, "let's go on a date tomorrow." "Really?" "Yes, it sounds too personal, but I have no other choice." She was happy for that words. "Thank you, sir." And she eats awful.

Next morning she comes out from the room. "I wonder if he's up yet. I hope he didn't change his mind." Then she goes to near the door. There he opens the door and comes out. He looks like shining star, she looks him like that with wondering. "It may be just a stimulation, but I thought I should dress properly for a date." "Yes, that's a great attitude." And she gives claps to him with smile. "But are you going out like that, Miss Lilly?" "Yes, I thought he'd hate if I go out like this to watch a movie with him." With a dance, she shows her dress to him. "What do you think? Do I look awful?" he thinks for a while and says, "instead of this, why don't you put on that reddish brown shirt? You should go with that, it's a little bit tackier, there are spots here and there, and the neck is stretched out too. How can I put this? Yes, you looked pretty awful." "I see. Then I'll wear that when I go out with him." "And you'll look careless if you put on your sneakers while stepping on the back as always. He may find you more unlikable." "I see. Thank you for your advice." "Shall we?" "Okay."

They goes to restaurant "sir, I'm about to show you the person of excess eating. I hope this won't become a problem in our relationship." He nods his head. "If I put you off a bit too much, call a time out." "okay." By serving herself she speaks out, "this is the best restaurant near our collage, but no matter how good it is, if I do quickly on this aggressively, don't you think I'll look awful? Watch this." Then she starts eating like beast... "Hay, miss Lilly." She looks at him. "Why don't you just eat noodle dish?" "Sorry?" "I watched you eat noodles last time. You got the sauce all over your mouth, and you slurped on the noodles very loudly. It might be more off-putting than this dish." "I see." "And you take a bite of your picked radish and leave the eaten once in your bowl. It seemed quite selfish too, so that could be off-putting." "Thanks for the great tips." She feels some awful and closes a bowl where all eaten bones were kept with hand." They goes to café after complete of eating. "Thank you for your help today, sir." "I'm glad I could be of help." The she takes coffee naturally by slurring it. "That was hot." "Right, when you drink hot drinks, you tend to slurp a lot. I think you should show such uncultured behavior too. And you should call your friend when you're with him. I overheard your call once, and it seemed like you were using all kinds of vulgar language such as, jerk, idiot, I'll kill you, and more. That could all be off-putting, so... "She gets disappointed. "What's wrong?" "Now I hear everything you said, there's no need for me to try so hard. I just have to be myself. I'm the human person of the word unlikable." "That's not what I meant. I'm sorry, miss Lilly. I shouldn't have focused on helping..." "No. then shall we go home? I think that was enough." She gets sad and se moves from there with bad mood. Then they both are on the way to home. Suddenly on way she looks archery center, "hay" then she goes there and looks off all dolls and so many are playing archery and trying to win dolls. Then he goes to Lilly, "do you want to give it a try?" "No, it's really though to shoot for ten points, actually." "It is?" "Yes. My brother is an archer, and he said it's not like the real one." he goes to the point where shoot was done then he makes try to shoot it. Lilly goes near to him. Then he gives one shot that he gets 10pointrs. Lilly gets shocked by his performance and looks for other shot and he gives 10 points for second shot too, she gets amazed, and when he is going to give a position to 3rd shot, she takes the feeling of playing archery with exiting, then he gets 3rd shot 10points. "All right! That was amazing. You're really good." She claps for it. "As I mentioned, I've once served as a military officer." "Yes, you're right, you did. I knew it.' He makes 4th shot too. "Here are your prizes." "Thank you." 'I'm sorry for making you upset today. Please accept my apology." "You're trying to win favor with these stuffed animals? If you thought I'd fall for something like these" she suddenly shows thumb finger. "You were right on!" by seeing to doll. 'God, this is so cute. Right, what if I smiled like a fool in front of him? Do you think that might be off-putting?" then she gives a smile and shows him. "You shouldn't smile like that." "Why not? Do I look too awful?" "You'll look pretty. Let's go, then." "What was that? He's attracting me, he's indeed a fox." Then they leave the place to home.

When they about to enter the house a person comes very fast and accidentally touches her then she suddenly fell sick with heavy stomach ache. Then peter takes her to bed and he sits beside her. "Are you all right, Miss Lilly?" "No, I'm not okay. I even had you touch me. Why can't I seem to get better?" "I'm sorry, but please excuse me." Then he touches her stomach. "What are you doing?" "The closer I am to the stone, the faster you'll get better." "What?" she feels better now and says "wait, you're right. Your hands must be medicinal. But I'm going to start flexing my tummy, so don't talk to me." Then she stops breathing to get flex, and says, "You already know a lot about me, but I want my body fat to remain a secret." "Hay, miss Lilly. You've worked out before, haven't you?" after saying this he laughs for it. "I can hear my privacy shattering in pieces." Later he removes his hand from her stomach and she gets relieved. "Do you feel better now?" "Yes." "Oh, god that almost killed me. It was unbelievably painful." "When you go out, you have to call me right away if anything happens." If I call, will you run over right away?" "Of course. I should protect you. Okay, then good night." "Good night"

Next morning she can't find her mobile that she is getting late to collage, and she comes out from the room and asks Mr. Peter. "Sir, did you see mobile I lost it." "No." "Oh, okay, can you lend me your mobile I will call to my mobile, to find it out." Then he gives his mobile to her and she makes call her mobile then she finds it "sir you deleted my contact?" "I didn't. I have never saved it." "Oh, I see." She is gives mobile to him, he is about to take it but, she takes it back, "I want you to save it though. I case of emergency." "Okay" then, she saves her number in his mobile. Then she accidentally sees contacts list. There was no number have been saved it was empty. "Why is there no one in your contacts?" "Because there is no one." "Not even family?" "No." "Not even friends?" "Not really." "Don't you have slightly known person?" "Are you done using it?" "But..." he takes his mobile and leaves.

Weekend the day now, she goes to meet Sameer and she makes awful day for him. She eats very awful and laughs awful as his things she got mad and he leaves her. Later she call peter "hello," "Miss Lilly?" "Sir, the days very awesome, we made it he left me without saying a word." "That's great." "Yes." "When you are coming then." "Right now I will be back." "Okay."

After she reaches home they both will be having dinner, she brings, goat blood to him and ice-cream to him. "Miss Lilly why you bought this?" You like ice-cream and goat blood to eat so I bought it to you." "Really?" "Yes." "Thank you." They both start eating. Then she goes to get some salt, when she just goes, a message will arrive to her mobile, mr.peter looks to the message, ["I'm sorry you I left without saying, so are you free tomorrow? Let's catch a movie." (Sameer).]

Next day she gets ready very formally and good looking. She moves to Mr. Peter where he was trimming the trees. "Are you going somewhere?" "Yes, I have to meet someone." "Okay. Don't be too late." "Okay, I'll be back." Then she leaves. Peter stands there and feel some stands there for a while thinking of something.

At night peter was waiting for Lilly that it's getting late. Then she comes there, "I'm home." "You're back." "I'm a little late, sir." "I thought you ran off with my marble." "I wouldn't!" "I'm kidding. But still, I thing we need a curfew." "A curfew?" "So that we won't be worried. Please be on home by 10PM from now on. If we break the rule, the Wi-Fi of the said person's room will be cut off." She gets shocked and shays, "hay, wait. The Wi-Fi? Wi-Fi is like the life of the modern man. I'd rather have you punish me!" "Punish you? So you're already thing of coming home lately?" "No, it's not that I'm already thinking about it." "Then." "I'm saying that there are emergencies. Why should I have to keep a curfew I'm my 20s, which I ignored even in high school, I want to back out of this contract. How much do I repay you." Then he looks at het silently with no expression. Then she says, "I'll come home early." "Okay, go and get some rest." She disappointedly moves to her room. When she closes door there gets a loud sound. Then he looks there, Lilly slowly comes and by fearing she says, "It was the wind that shut the door hard." "Yes, I know." Then she slowly goes in. then peter laughs for her behavior.

There comes a day that when Lilly goes to collage all people looks at her. She was suspicious and thinks "why all are looking on me" then, Swetha comes to her "what happened, why all are looking at me." "Sameer and his friends made on you bet with 1lakh, that you can fall for him, and they are saying you intentionally make him avoided to get him back." She will be strong for that. Later Mr. Peter senses something bad about her. When she was living collage to home it turns dark in parking area but she silent stands there with sad ness. Then peter comes in front of her, after seeing him she bursts in to tears and cries on hugging him. "they have bet on me, I'm not a thing to bet>' she cries more, then peter says. "It's okay, don't cry I'm here for you, okay? Let's go. Then, she sees him with watery eyes and shows him hands, "I want to fly now, please." He laughs for that, "last time you said that's the last one." Then she gets disappointed and keeps flowing water in her eyes. Then he takes her in to his arms and starts flying. She smiles little and holds him tightly and falls in to sleep in his arms. He takes her to her bed, and comes back to hall and turns on TV.

At morning she comes out from her room and look for peter, she finds him in the garden sitting there thinking of something. She gives ice-cream to Mr. Peter and she also has one. Then Mr. Peter staring on to her, "why are you looking at me like that?" "It looks like you feel better now, so imp relived." "It's thanks to you, sir. Yesterday could've been the worst day of my life, but thanks to you, it because a little funnier, thank you, really." He smiles for the words. Then Lilly receives a message, she open it and looks it. "What? Only he looks good." Then, peter peeks in to her mobile, and then she shows to him. "My brother sent me our picture. But I don't look in any of these, why did he send me these?" he don't understand what's about and looks at her. "Right, it's that day when I went out to meet someone. I went to watch my brothers match." "You went on that day to meet your brother." "yes." He smiles for the thing. "Why did you just smile?" "I smiled?" "Yes." "What?" "What?" then, she gets a bite of ice-cream where she's gets it on her mouth? He smiles for her looking and wipes it with his hands, she looks at him for a while, and "you have some here." "Oh, you are so ancient. You can't stand to see something that isn't neat." He smiles for the words, and Lilly feels some uneasy, and staring him for a while when they are going inside the house. She goes to her room and falls on bed and thinks, "OMG, he'll be a great person once he comes a human.

When she was having some water suddenly feels stomach ache. There come peter, "what's wrong, miss Lilly?" "My stomach suddenly began to ache." The then thinks and asks. "Sir, what's today date?" "I believe it's the 2nd." Then she looks in to her mobile calendar. On the date 2nd it was written as [period]. Then she here some notice for herself that, ["hi, I came back this month to destroy your character and happiness."]. She fells disappointed, "sir, I'm expecting my condition to worsen today, so I'll go back and get some rest." "What do you mean, you're expecting it to worsen?" she leaves without answering.

He will be waiting for to come out, and looks in to his watch its 3PM she was still in, he slowly goes near to her door and knocks the door. "Are you alright' Miss Lilly? Are you sure you don't need lunch? Should I get some food?" "please." By hearing this he gets worried, "I'm coming in. miss Lilly." And he enters in rush, and looks her by sitting beside her, "I want pizza, ice-cream, noodles, please." She says this with weak voice. "I'm sorry, miss Lilly. I didn't know you were this sick." "Why should you be sorry? It's not like you're my estrogen." "Sorry?" "Period cramps." "I see, and then what can I do for you? I'll go get a hot water bottle bad, food and some water." He rushes out and brings all the things in excess. She comes to dining table and eats like a kid by showing her eating to peter, "I'm sick, but it tastes good." "Take it easy, Miss Lilly. And I got something for you. There are supplements and these are painkillers and these are your favorite snacks." She excitedly laughs and says "I'm sure you will be a good human." "What?" "Including the guys in my collage and the guys I hear from the news, there are so many evil men in this world. To be honest, when I met you, I thought it was like a fantasy, but these days, I think humans are more like a fantasy. Anyway, you are way more human than those weirdo's. It's not easy to be nice to someone without expecting anything in return. Anyway how you know all this about to take medicine and eating more food?" "well, I have seen some of girls are very severe in stomach ache in past as they were poor they are going on starving them just becoming weak and dying early age, then I understand that they need to eat as they like and to get rest, apart from that I don't want you to die at early stage." She gets staring on him for a while. Later she goes to her bed and takes supplements. Mr. Peter comes to her, "does it hurt a lot?" "It does. I don't usually have menstrual cramps this bad when I'm on my period. This time, my whole body feels weak. It's strange." He feels bad for her and looks at her for some time. "I'll take some rest now." "Okay, take good rest, Miss Lilly." "Good night."

Mr. Peter meets the girl who was fox "is your gender identity the reason why you haven't collected all the energy yet?" "Watch your mouth. Please, let's not make any problem" "I'm not sure, I'm too curious. What's happening yesterday?" "She is sick, so I have helped her," "no wonder why she's sick. The stone is stealing her energy. But I wasn't asking how she's doing. I was asking why you're doing this." "What are you trying to say?" "One mistake is enough. When you said you started to live with a human, I was worried you might mess it up because of your personal feelings. In the end, the stone will steal all her energy and she will either die or may be close to death. And it will be torture for you to watch that in front of you. Still, I thought it might be okay. Because you're peter. But you seem to have started to get attached to her. Think about it. Has it ever ended well, when we had feelings? "She leaves the place, then, he recalls the past that a girl was dying in his arms where he was crying for her. "She is right, getting attached to her won't do any good.

From next day he avoids her. She searches for him to say that she was going to collage and finally she finds him and says, "Hi, sir, I'm going to college." "Okay, you don't need my permission for that." "What? But you were worried about it before." "I know you can take care of yourself." "Yes, that's right but..." "You don't need to tell Mr. everything unless it's important. We are nothing more than two people who accidentally got involved with each other." then he lefts the place. Lilly was upset by his behavior. "Why he is avoiding me? What wrong I have done?" the she will leave to collage.

Later when she was coming collage, as she was sad she recalls some memories with him, when she is passing through restaurant she find Mr. Peter having seat. He also look at her, he finds that she was about to cry, and stares her for a while, then she comes to peter. "Miss Lilly?" then she takes a seat, "sir. Just like you said, I know we accidentally got involved with each other. So I know we don't need to care about each other, but you know what? I can't do that. I wish we can be like we used to be. What should I do?" "Miss Lilly..." "You said you feel comfortable around me. You said I was okay, you said the stone wasn't the only reason why you were nice to me. How could a human change his mind like..." she suddenly stops saying because he was not human, again she speaks out, and "do you think you can just change your mind because you're not a human? You can't just avoid me when we were doing fine." Then she starts crying. "Miss Lilly, I said that because I concluded that it might be better that I stay away from your life. But it looks like it rather concerned you more. I'm sorry." "If you're sorry, let's be like we used to be. I'll come back and sit, so talk to me and worry about me like you used to do."

She moves some far and comes back to peter, then she takes the seat. Then she silently looks at her and Lilly makes a sound to talk something. "How was it with that guy?" "It was alright." "What's wrong, did he push you again?" "No, he was nice to me." "I think he have special feeling on you." "Actually, I'm not sure. I doubt this is true, but if, by any chance, he has special feelings for me, I think it's strange. Because he just made a bet on me." Then he says some sayings that "you like someone means, that you are misunderstanding that person in your own way." "then she feels something special when he was saying some this like, "to him, she seemed so beautiful, so seductive, so different from ordinary people, that he could not understand, why no one was as distributed as he, by clicking of her heels on the paving stones, why no one else's heart was wild, with the breeze stirred by the sighs of her veils, why everyone did not go mad with the movements of her braid, the flight of her hands, the gold of her laughter, he could not understand, why anyone wouldn't fall in love with her." Then they both look them with some special feeling. Later they are just spending time, she gives a message to a group that who are present in group are jinn and swetha along with her, [guys, listen up. This is my friend's story.] They both think "it's her, it's her story." [Her heart suddenly starts to pound, she had tough time breathing, and then she felt airheaded as if she's walking on clouds. What does this mean?] [Jinn: "arrhythmia?"] Then swetha personally messages to jinn. "Stop fooling around, this is once in a lifetime opportunity to make Lilly fall in love." "I'm sorry, I'm sorry." [Swetha: "when did you... no, wait. When did your friend have those feelings?"] [Lilly: "well, when she was just with somebody"] [Swetha: "I think your friend fell for that somebody."] [Lilly: "no, that can't be it."] [Jinn: "you said it's your friend. How do you know?"] Then she stops texting. And she goes to bed.

Later, peter says "let's go home now". "okay." After going to some place she excitedly says, "Lets teleport to home." "no. let's walk." "Please I want to teleport." "No." "Yes." "no." then she roughly says "I want teleport, if not I won't come." Then, she sits on the road, in front of him, "gets up lets go, why are you behaving like a child." "I'm not a child understand." Then he picks her up in his arms and just gets teleport to his house. She was very happy that she was shouting and laughing like. "I got teleported home" she makes house so loud. He can't stop her and just sitting on sofa by closing his ears.

He completes the writing some project work in library with those three partner girls and completes cork and about to go home, one of them says, "Great work. See you at the next meeting." When 2 girls leave she calls peter, "excuse me, Mr. Peter. Well, you know. We'll have to go out for field study soon, so why don't we discuss the schedule, over dinner with me sometime?" "Next time." "Yes, I would like to schedule when exactly that next time will be." "I thought dancing around was my way of showing courtesy, but I should probably make myself clear. I'm not looking to eat dinner with you. I'm sorry? I don't feel comfortable dining with somebody else." Then she leaves the place. She says, "That was hurtful."

When Lilly was picking up books in library, there comes Sameer "I want go someplace with you." "Sorry I cant." "Why?" "I want to get home early. And I can't go like you people, who make bet on girls." "Oh, at least can we spend some time in restaurant?" "sorry." This conversation was seen by jinn, and he goes to swetha where she was studying in library. "Hay, I saw this on my way here. Sameer was totally coming onto Lilly, but Lilly kept pushing him away like a bouncing ball. What if Sameer gives up on her? Let's ask them to grab a drink, and then we can help them get together." "Let's not do any stuff and stay still, okay?" why should we stay still? Let's call Sameer 1st." "Hay stop that!" there is another guy she likes. I have seen him, when they are having dinner at restaurant." "You've seen what?" "He didn't seem like just known person. Her face was... I think it was the guy she talked to me about." "She talked to you?" "Last week, she was warned things seemed distant with this person." "Really? I haven't heard anything. Why didn't she tell me?" he gets disappointed. "I'm sure there was a reason. Anyway, we should wait until she tells us. Don't act like you know something. Okay? Will you?" "Yes, I'll do that."

Then, jinn was passing through a café in the collage, there Lilly spots him and asks him, "Jinn, want some coffee?" "No." "What's with this cold response?" "What about it? What do you mean?" "You obviously look annoyed. Stop piling up and tell me." "Aren't you the one, who should be telling me something?" "What?" "I'm a little disappointed. There is nothing I haven't told you. You know everything about my ex-girlfriend, the ex before that, the one before... forget it, I told you everything I want too ashamed to share with my brother. But I guess you didn't feel that way. Bye" "hay, jinn. Then she thinks, "What was that?"

They all go to class and have seats, and then Lilly asks swetha, "What's with him?" "What?" "He said I didn't tell him something. What could it be?" "I'm not sure." Anhh okay." Then swetha secretly messages him [swetha: "hay, I told you not to get so childish."] [Jinn: whatever, I'm disappointed. What can I do?] After going home, she messages to jinn [jinn: hay! Are you seriously doing this?"] [Jinn: what?] Then, she gets angry in peaks and calls him. He lifts the call, "hello?" then she shouts, "Hello, my foot. What your problem? What it is?" "You'll pop my eardrum! Just leave me alone. Give me some time to be set." "Are you getting deaf? Why do you need some time? What are you disappointed about? Tell me. Tell me now." Then, he hang up the call, Lilly gets angry to peaks and shout like that house gets break "you!" Mr. Peter who was sitting with reading book in hall gets scared by that notice and says, "Gosh, darn it!" "You jerk! You idiot!" and Mr. Peter was more scared. Then she will come out and take ice cubed to her mouth and controls her anger. "Are you alright, miss Lilly?" "I'm sorry, sir. That must've been loud." 'Is something bad going on?" "Well, jinn is anger at me, but I don't know why. I wanted to talk, but he avoids me. He ignores my texts and hung up on me too." "You two looked very close. That must be disconcerting." "Yes. As you know, I have a younger brother. But ever since I met him I felt like I had two younger brothers. We were close like real siblings. Why is he doing this to me? Sir, will you come out with me?" casually he says, "sure." Then he gets surprise, "Sorry?"

They take a ride out "why don't we have some ice-cream that we love so much?" "No, I don't feel like." Lately peter looks a small palm wine center. "Do you want to grab a drink?" "A drink?" "Humans seem to drink alcohol to forget their problems. I figured you might need that now." "It's okay. I'm not supposed to drink" "you haven't been drinking until now, and I'm with you today, so I think it'll be okay." "But still..." "Let's go." He grabs her hand and runs towards it. They will be having a seat.

"Miss Lilly, the 'idealism' says one must stop drinking while one feels good. I think we should set limits before we start drinking. How much alcohol can you take?" "Three bottles of palm wine." He gets shocked, "seven... why don't we order just one bottle?" "two." He laughs for her childish way, "Are you making a deal with me now?" "Well, if we're going to drink anyway, we should drink until we feel good just like 'the idealism' says." "Just half bottle of palm wine will hardly touch my organs." "But you haven't been drinking for a while, so..." "Come on. I know my liver. One bottle of palm wine can't make it drunk." And she makes an order, "ma'am, I'd like to order two bottles of palm wine and omelet." "okay." She was very happy and waiting for the order.

She starts drinking, "I thought I wouldn't be able to drink any for one year." "Miss Lilly. You're not going to pretend to be down when you want to drink, are you?" "That's a very good tip." They both laughs for it. Then she will be going on drinking with no stop. "Alcohol is the best." She behaves differently that she makes all colors of emotion; he gets shocked and finally smiles. "Sir, why are you smiling?" "Well, watching you fascinate me, one moment you're happy, the next you are upset. One moment you laugh, the next, you frown." "Are you saying I can't control my emotions?" "That's not what I'm saying. I like it. Miss Lilly, I have lived a long time. When you live for such a long time, everything feels like just a season that will eventually pass. And everything feels meaningless. But you seem true to yourself every moment. I like... your honesty." She smiles and fall asleep all of sudden by saying "I love you." Then peter will be on her side and catches her.

Later, in the morning, she wakes up and recalls what happened last night, the she was uncomfortable with that word and she try to escape form him, she slowly gets ready to collage and slowly steps out without giving sight to peter, when she was just to step out he suddenly appears in front of her, she gets scared and shouts very scary. "How... but you were there just now." "I teleported. I haven't done it for a while. Can we talk for a moment?" "no. let's talk later." She slowly tries to walk out by saying "later in the evening. Actually, tomorrow. Or a few months later." He blocks her way, the she looks at him like a caught thief. "It won't take longer than ten minutes" they will have a seat; peter speaks out "after hearing what you said last night, I gave it a lot of thought." "Oh, that... I was just carried away by the mood. I wasn't serious or anything." "Still, if I had known it, I would have been more considerate. I thought about what I could do about it, and I prepared something." "What? "Then he brings some omelet and gives it to her. "If I had known you liked omelet so much, I would have taken it into consideration, when we bought groceries or ate out. I'm sorry." Then he recalls the last night word that, she looks to omelet and says I love you to it. He gets that thing instead of him. She was disguised with it "what with the face?" "Oh. Never mind." She murmurs for herself, "Well, I'm glad he didn't get it."

When a girl was crossing the road, she finds out a pen was coming from the opposite to the wall, she picks it up and observes it where she gets afraid because blood stain was present on it. Then she gives a look towards the side where pen was scrolled from, it gets scared to death that a person was dead who was killed cruelly.

A fox girl who turned in to human was looking on to the news, ["a person was murdered by cutting off corpse limbs occurs again, considering the crime has been committed in the middle of downtown, the abdomen of the corpse has been brutally abused, and none of the crimes were caught. The abused parts of the corpse are identical by CCTV or cameras. The police have announced they will carry out the investigation based on the assumption it's a serial murdered."] "Could this be..." she gets worried and hurries up towards the peter, on the way she calls peter, "did you see the news? There is something fishy about it." "What do you mean?" "It doesn't seem like it could have been done by a human. Why don't you do some research on it? Who knows it's related to us..." "You have many problems, but your biggest problem is that you stick your nose into everything." Then he hangs up the call.

Later, a person was observing behind the Lilly at every moment for days after murder news comes up.

Lilly have a seat at collage and thinking of herself about the stone to get removed, there comes swetha, "what's up? What are you thinking about?" "Nothing." "Is this because of jinn? Lilly, I'm sorry. It's because of me." "Because of you?" "Well... actually, I recently saw you getting dinner with someone." "What?" "And I told jinn about it. You said it was your friend, but we know you. You were obviously talking about yourself. But you wouldn't tell us about it and make more secrets from us. And jinn seem upset about it." "I see." "By the way, the man you were with that day... he is the man you talked about before, right? The man you were afraid was avoiding you." "Yes." "How do you know him?" "I just know him." "Are you seeing him?" "I'm not seeing him. Actually I don't know. I know I shouldn't, but I seem to develop feelings for him." "Why shouldn't you?" "I don't know how to explain. You wouldn't believe me anyway" "okay, since you don't want to talk about it, I won't ask you anymore. But if you can't even tell, if he's someone you're seeing or someone you just know, don't like him so much. It's only bad for you. Then she thinks about it, "Now I think about it, I don't know how to define this relationship." She just moves from there and thinking of it while walking, "he is not just someone I know. But he's not someone I'm seeing either. I might be some misfortune that happened to him." Then a person was watching her back silently.

When peter was driving someplace he goes in to news, ["this is the next news. The police have done an postmortem on the women in her 20s brutally murdered in the middle of downtown, and announced that the cause of death was organ damage and heavy bleeding caused by stab on the abdomen. They have concluded that the victim has stabbed alive and based on the shape of the cut on the abdomen, it is presumed that she was not attacked with a weapon but bitten, which is making this case more and more of a mystery."] Then he remembers girl words about the news. Then he suddenly looks on to a colony road, where Lilly was going to home, "Miss Lilly?" And he looks a person following her, he worries and follows them, when they were going person gets suddenly disappear. Lately he follows her to home, when she reaches home she stands in front of gate and thinks that, "That Mr. Fox might think of me as no one but someone who made a contract with him, or just some misfortune that happened to him...that I might be no one to him, that depresses me."

When they reach home, at middle of night peter looks after her room, but she won't respond to him and he gets worries and teleports to her room but he can't find her. He comes out from her room and massages her, [peter: where are you, miss lily? I will come to pick you up if you went out if you get late.] She won't replay to his message; he senses something fishy about her and uses his power to find her. He finds something and walks towards his secret tunnel, there he finds Lilly, sitting on the steps in very upset mood. "Miss Lilly. What are you doing here?" "Sir. I've been sitting here like this since 10 p.m. sharp. Technically, I didn't break the curfew." "Does that matter now? I said, what are you doing here?" then he cover-up her with his coat. "You said you wouldn't worry me." "I'm sorry. Didn't want to go home like this. I really wanted to have some alcohol, but I didn't, because I promised you I wouldn't." "Did something happen, Miss Lilly?" "Sir. You said I seemed true to myself every moment and you liked my honesty, so I'll be honest. You have met many people and experienced many things, so I'm sure nothing is hard for you. But I'm not like you. I'm the opposite of cool. We're supposed to be just two people living together by contract, but I can't keep my private public life separate because I'm not as cool as you. What I'm saying is, no matter how you think of me, you are special and significant to me. So special that I can give up all alcohol and food that I like." He gets surprised and looks at her with thinking "dishonesty cannot beat honesty, never." "Me too. Miss Lilly, you are special to me too." They look each other for a while. "Do you remember? Everything feels like a season that passes by after living for a long period just as I have. At first, you were like that too. You were just a passing shower. But, I'm still standing in the rain; it's difficult to explain our relationship apart from the marble and the contract. But to me, you are...special." "And by that, you mean..." "You're like a family to me." "Sorry?" "I've never had any family, but I always thought it would be like this to have a family. Well, it would be weird to say you're like my daughter." He smiles for his words.

Then Lilly gets shocked for it.

Next morning, he prepares coffee; she comes out from her room. “Are you going to college, Miss Lilly? You should grab a cup of coffee.” She silently comes to him and takes the coffee very hardly and drinks up firstly. “Hay, it smells nice. It’s like coffee you get at a café. I almost gave you my credit card to pay it, uncle.” “UN...” “I gave this thought. I thought it would be better if I called you my uncle instead of sir. Because I’m like a daughter to you.” “Miss Lilly...” “And on a good day, feel free to give me some pocket money too. Because I’m like a daughter to you. Then bye, uncle.” Then she lives the place. “Did I do something wrong again? Let’s look back on what I did, peter.

Fox women who turned in to human reaches to peter home. “I came to share my win-win scenario. I need your help. To be exact, your magic, but whatever.” “What do you want? I’ve played long enough, and I got sick of spending money. I tried so hard to become a human, but it wasn’t such a big deal now that I am one. That’s why, I’m thinking of going to this place called collage.” “Collage?” “Yes, a university.” “When it took you 80years to learn 1000 Indian characters?” “Exactly. I’m sick and tired of how you look down on me. I want to live the rest of my life as women of intellect.” Then he looks to coffee cut which he was having it, “it smells nice” “really? Then I’d like a cup” he won’t care about her words and having coffee. “Give it a good thought. This isn’t a bad deal for you. Aren’t you nervous, anxious, and sleepless these days? The stone finally began to turn blue, so what if something happens? You must feel very troubled. Don’t you need someone to keep an eye on her? Just to be safe and clear.”

Later after giving a thought about girl’s words and incidents happened, he says to him, “I have no other choice.” Then he massage to the girl, [peter: let’s do that. Just to be safe and clear.] “He really took my bait.

Next day she goes to college, and everyone pays attention towards her. Then she thinks, “Do I look miserable?” on the other side jinn and his other friend talking, “darn it!” other person says, “hay, wait. Look over there.” Jinn heart gets flutter after seeing the girl, she walks towards him and speaks out, “hay, I need to ask you a question, where is the department of history?” “Right, yes. Go down this way, walk past the main library, then take a right, you’ll see a huge building. There are all kinds of snack bars and you know, those, vending machines and stuff. So if you keep going down that way. Well... should I just walk you there?” he gets shivering while he is saying all these. “Will you?” “Sure. Come with me.”

On the way they meet Lilly and swetha. There Lilly and swetha looks on her, then jinn speaks up, “her name is hansika. She’s from other city and she came as an exchange student” swetha looks at her and says, “Hi, I’m kajal of OU university, the top student of history.” They both shake their hands with fighting face. Lilly speaks out. “Hi, I’m just Lilly.” They shake with their hands. She senses something about Lilly and splits out, “nice to meet you. Let’s be good friends.” “Sure.”

They all reach the class, hansika seats beside Lilly, then she messages to peter, [hansika: I just met her. The kid you live with.] when professor was taking attendance list hansika stares only Lilly at all time, Lilly observes her and speaks to herself, “why does she keep staring at me like that?” later class gets boring to all students and do their activities without listening.

Lilly reaches home at night, at 3 a.m. when peter comes out from his room, he spots Lilly at dining table eating all snack stuff like a ghost, and he gets scared about her behavior. “Excuse me, Miss Lilly. If you eat late night snacks too often...” “No way, eating something at 3 a.m. should be considered breakfast. My mom said I should eat well in the morning.” Later at 8 a.m. she runs out with shorts from her room, then she asks peter that, “I ran out of my lotion. May I use yours?” “Its fine, but you want to use...” she runs off to his room even though he did not complete his words, and brinks a lotion from his room, then she takes seat in front of him, “do you want to use men’s lotion?” “Who cares? It’s all the same.” Then she applies like a kid. “Soft and moist.” Later she rushes to collage with wired dress. “I’m going collage.” “You’re leaving like that again?’ she even not tied up with her shoe lays. “yes.” He gets shocked about her behavior and smiles at it.

At collage the three friends meet up at canteen and having breakfast. Then jinn speak up, “why are you picking on your food? Start eating like a pig.” Lilly splits out. “I told something of a love confession day before yesterday,” both swetha and jinn gets shocked for it, “but he said I’m like his daughter. It means I’m turned down, right?” jinn say “you did. You were turned down but into the outer universe. I’ve never been turned down that harshly before. He couldn’t have taken you for women if he said you’re a...” then swetha kicks him to stop talking. “I’m leaving.” Swetha speaks out, "Lilly, you should finish before you..." Lilly leaves the place. "You idiot. Why did you say something like that? She even has not eaten up." "I just felt bad for her." Swetha leaves him with angry face.

Later in the evening, jinn having dinner with Lilly in a restaurant, where peter also comes there, they will be part from different tables because of jinn. Jinn asks Lilly, "hay, you got just 70% grade in last semester." "Lunch, okay, you know I don't think off grades." A person from other tables listens it and speaks out, "what? 70% grade let me give you one last piece of advice as a senior in life. Instead of shopping for clothes, buy some books to add a line to your resume. Instead of putting highlighter makeup on, go highlighters on your book. Do you get what I'm saying?" Lilly feels uneasy that all conversation was listing by peter. Then jinn speaks, "if you don't know someone's dream, then don't mess up with them, you jerk get out." Then, he was about to leave the restaurant, peter uses his power and makes him to get fell down. Then all laughs at him, then he runs off from there. Lilly looks at peter where he was smiling for his thing. Then, jinn says "okay, I'm getting late I need to pick up brother I will go first, you go safely okay? Bye." He leaves the place. Later both Lilly and peter walks out, on the way peter calls her, "hay, Miss Lilly, miss Lilly, can you tell me?" "Tell you what?" "Why were you offended when I said you're like a daughter to me? Please tell me." "Yes, right. I see." She hesitates to say it, "well." "Miss Lilly. As you know the only thing I can do is mimicking what humans do. So my choice of words may not have been proper. But what I wanted to tell you on that day wasn't that you're like a daughter. I meant that you're special. Over 1000 years of my life. I never took in anybody like they're my family. It took me lots of courage, to say what I shared with you. Could you understand what I was trying to say?" then she speaks in for herself, "if you continue to be nice to me, I can't get over you." "Miss Lilly, you don't look..." "Unhh, I was just reminded of what that guys said to be. He said it in an off-putting way, but it was all true. I already know how important this time in my life is. Instead of worrying about a job. I loved studying history, so I did that. But people keep telling me to face the reality." "Miss Lilly, there's something I need to show you." He holds her hand and teleports to a place called historical museum, "wait, what is this place? Isn't this placed closed? Are we allowed to be here?" "Well, only if you'll keep it a secret." "In that case, this might be my only opportunity in life." Then both will be having fun by watching them, she gets excited for everything she looks off. Peter feels elated and happy by seeing her happy. "Gosh, white porcelains. So cute. Have you ever used this in real time, sir?" "Of course. You're calling me sir again." "right." And she hesitantly moves from there and looks other things. He smiles for her shyness and follows her. With so much of excitement she hugs all the places where things was covered by glass wall, they both spends a time there with more affection. "By the way, why do you like history so much?" "I think I started to like it because of historic dramas, my brother and I spent a lot of time alone at home, so we watched TV a lot. I used to find museums boring, but after learning about the palace of illusions by chitra Banerjee divakaruni, his journal touched my heart. They say, 'love comes like lightning and disappears the same way. If you are lucky, it strikes you right. If not, you'll spend your life yearning for a man you can't have.' But, I think the more you know, the more you get to like it." "Do you know when is the first time I saw your smile?" he remembers that when they were in the tunnel. "It was in the basement." "I see." "Miss Lilly, living a long life, I've learned one thing from seeing numerous people. When you like something a lot, you'll be led in that direction. So I'm sure your wish will come true. That guy who said about your grade earlier kept saying he's more experienced in life. I've lived a longer life, so I should know better than him." "That's why you took me here." "I don't want you to give up on what you like." "is it really okay that I don't give up?" he nodes his head like yes, when are looking for each other, there a voice comes from outside "is anybody there?" there comes security checking the museum, then peter uses his power to turn off all lights, then he drags her hand and hides under the table. Security was going on checking every corner of the museum. Then slowly by murmuring Lilly speaks out. "Sir, foxes also gets hide when they thinks when they are going too caught." And laughs for it, the she plays with him under the table like she tries to throw out from hiding and suddenly she misses her kick towards him that she gets fell on him, they feels something special and his power loses his control and teleports to the place they have come from.

They both get up and take walk to their home. "I'm glad he didn't find us" "it would've been good if we could look around more. What a shame." "It's ok. I saw enough."

Later peter calls hansika, "what's up? You never call me." "Where are you?" "On a terrace in my room. I love heights. It's probably because I've seen watching over humans on the roof. You wouldn't know how beautiful city looks from here at night." "I think I do." He suddenly appears at her side, she gets startled, "goodness, you scared me. You can't just show up like that without discussing it with me." "Why did you meet her without discussing it with me?" "Are you talking about Lilly? I found no good reason to turn down a friend I made in collages. Plus, it's not like you have special feelings for her." "Let me ask you one thing. Why are you suddenly doing this to me?" "It will be your 1000th year soon, so I'm worried." "I don't think it's you place to worry about it." "That's upsetting. You know what relationship we have." "What relationship?" "A love-and-hate relationship. We are the only once in this world so I don't want to see you crushed. I managed it somehow, but you didn't handle it well to have someone special to you.

When Lilly was with their friends, her mom calls her, "hay, mom." "Lilly. You said you're staying at a friend's because of a project. What's the address?" "What? Why, all of a sudden?" "So I can send you the clothes we have left after the photo-shoot." "They are too experimental to wear anyway." "Anyway, text me the address." Then she hands up the call. Lilly thinks, "Oh, well. It's not like she'll fly here from the US." She sends peter address to her mom.

She gets another call from her brother Aman, "hay, Aman." "Did you get mom's call?" "Yes. She asked for my address so she can send me a package." "No, she's not. She's in the city now." "What?" "Gosh, why are you shouting, what's so surprising about that?" "Of course, I'm surprised. Why she is she in city? She didn't say anything." "She said she was on her way to city. And she's lying over in city because there had been an issue with the fight. But why didn't she tell you this and only ask for the address? Is she planning to make surprise visit?" "Hay, I've got to go now." He hangs up the call and says to their friends, "I should go." "Hay, why? Where are you going?" she hurry to go home. On the way, she calls peter, "yes, miss Lilly." "Sir, I'm in big trouble now." Suddenly her mobile was dead. "She looks worried to the mobile. On the other hand peter calls her, "Miss Lilly?"

Someone gives calling bell he goes to the door and opens it up by saying "Miss Lilly." After seeing her, "who are you?" "I'm lily's mother. Lilly is living here, right?" they will go into house and have seats, peter was little bit nervous. "I thought I might have come to the wrong place, because the house seemed too big and nice for a college student. Are you the owner of the house? How do you know Lilly?" "Well..." he thinks for himself, "a precious part of me is inside your daughter's stomach. This may sound like she's pregnant. I'm paying your daughter's tuition in exchange for her company. This may sound like we have an inappropriate relationship" "gosh, why are you nervous? Did I ask something hard to answer?" then he gets tense for her questions. There comes Lilly by running, "mom! mom! You didn't say you were coming." Peter gets relief foe Lilly presence, "let me explain this. So my original plan was to stay at my friends place but it was too small. So we decided to share a house." "Stop the fuss and sit down" "okay." Lilly takes a seat beside of peter. 'So you're sharing a house. So where's your friend?" they both says at a time that, Lilly says "she'll be back soon..." but peter says "she recently moved out..." they both shuts their mouth all of a sudden. "How long have you been living here? Again the both speak out at a time, that Lilly says, "it's only been a week." But peter says, "About a month." Again they both shut their mouth with tense. "So did you meet each other?" again they make mistake by responding at a same time with different answer like one says "on the internet..." and other says "a real estate agent..." then Lilly thinks "I'm doomed." She slowly speaks to peter, "where's your magic?" "You told me not to use..." "Come on do it." Peter tries to erase her memory for a moment, but nothing happens. Then he thinks off "I heard you couldn't use magic towards someone who is strong-minded, but..." then Lilly looks at peter with suspension, where peter nodes his head like it's not working then they both gets tensed for her mother. "Lilly, you know how much I hate lies." "Yes." "From now on, lying will only make this worse. Are you living with him?" peter splits out. "I can explain. It is true that she's staying at my house. But there hasn't been anything to worry about and there won't be." "I'm not worried. Whether it was weeks or months you've lived with her, so you should know that my daughter has quite a personality. I didn't even mean to scold her for living with you. I just hate lies." "I'll go now." Lilly was happy and says "are you leaving now?" "Don't you think you sound too excited?" Lilly and her mother walks out, Lilly say, "I'm sorry I didn't tell you about it, but really, it's not like what you think." "I believe you know what you are doing, but let me just say this one thing." "Okay." "I like it." "What? The house?" "Seriously? You have good taste just like your dad." "Seriously, it's not what you think." "It's not? I see. Then I wish it will be. Good luck. I'll go now." "Lilly gets shocked for words, "okay, bye. Call me when you arrive. Bye." Then her mom leaves the place in a cab. Lilly says for herself, "maybe I should have sent her off at the airport." When she turns back peter comes there, "I'll drive you to the airport." "What?" "If we hurry, you'll have some time to see her off."

They both reaches airport, Lilly comes first in to the airport, there comes Aman dashing Lilly calling mom! "Hay, what are you doing here?" Lilly says "I asked him to come with me to see you off." "Aman you said you had important training." "This is more important. You should've told me you were staying only for three hours. I didn't know you'd leave so early." By looking in to Aman clothes she says, "Hay, why do you look so... do you wash yourself?" "Of course. She's the one you want to harass about washing; she leaves her hair unwashed for three days." "That's to save shampoo. I care about this count's environment." "Wasn't it because you were homeless?" "Do you want to die?" "What?" "You are homeless." "Right." "You want to die. " "You never take showers." "I do." Then her mother smiles for their silly fighting, "I've got to go." Then Lilly asks, "When are you coming back?" Aman speaks out, "a sudden meet up and a sudden goodbye. I don't like this. We haven't met for a year." Then she goes close to them, "my Lilly, my Aman, you remember our family motto?" then they both says same word, "Live your life on your own." "And you know I believe you can do that." Then Lilly speaks up, "why are you saying that now?" "I wanted to say thank you for growing into great people. I don't feel comfortable leaving you two alone here either. But I have never regretted it, because I believe in you." Then they both hug her with affection. This was seen by peter from a distance. Lilly and peter takes a back to home.

On the way Lilly speaks up, "sir, it's been a hectic day, right? Thank you so much. I could see her off all thanks to you." "That's no problem. You must be sad though." "It feels a bit strange, but I guess that's what family is like. We may fight all the times, whenever something happens, we support each other. That's probably why thinking about them makes me feel safe." "So that's what family is like." "You have me. You said I was like your family; I want to be like family to you someone who supports you no matter what and makes you feel safe. Even after we take out the stone." She leaves the place and enters the house.

Later when he was standing at the window he thinks that which was said by hansika. Later he remembers past, [there was an attack by forest people on village people, a person was about to kill a women and a small kid in her arms, then there comes peter and kills him and protects them. From there all people will be having fight with peter he defeats all the people, on the other way people are attacking a girl and his father, when they are escaping a person comes up opposite to them and he kills her father in front of her, she gets scared and cries for her father. Person goes near to her to kill, and then peter saves her by killing him, "are you okay?" she cries full of heart broken for her father death. Peter moves towards fighting with enemies at night fight come to an end by defeating all of them. When he looks at her she is still crying for her father with high vocal voice that was giving a human feeling to peter.] Peter says for him, "I thought it was nothing. Insincere act of kindness. Meaningless affection. They were just what I do habitually, so I didn't think it was anything special, I could have saved her life, if I had taken the marble out and pretended nothing had happened. If I hadn't hesitated to take the marble out and erase all the memories. If I hadn't been afraid of being forgotten by her." In the past peter says to the girl, ["just think of this as a bad dream when you wake up, both your memories and pain will be gone." "Don't cry. This is not your fault, you just wanted to stay with me, I wish your dream comes true and meet someone to teach you, what it is like to be together." He gets shocked for her words, "did you know it all this time?" then she gives marble to him. She dies in his arms and he gets broke down to tears.] "Never let myself fall in love with her..." but it was too late when I realized my mistake. I might have just wanted to ignore how mutually opposed it was to me to have someone special. It was just a coincidence of marble get in to her, and that could have been it that should have been it, she has her family, her life and her people. Is it fair that I keep her by my side? Just because she makes my life more interesting and less lonely? Just because I'm afraid I might disappoint her? Until when? Until something really bad happens to her?

At morning Lilly comes out from her room "sir, you're up early." ["Today is the day, I should let her go."] "Why do you look at me like that?" "Miss Lilly, are you free tonight?" "What?" "I thought we should grab a cup of coffee at a nice café." "Sounds good. I'd love to"

Later in collage after the class Lilly asks jinn, "what are you doing? What is that?" "I have been making a list of great places to go with my future girlfriend. I never know where to take girls." "Hay, doesn't this place look great? It's quite and desolate, so you can solely focus on each other." Lilly was curious in that place and drags his mobile and looks in to it, "where is this place?" she message peter [Lilly: "sir! I found this new popular café. I'll be there right after my classes. See you at 8PM. click to view on a map." Peter: "I'll take off soon too"] when they have on this conversation a fox was peeping in to peter through the window.

When peter gets ready and to get off to cafe will be going to turn of TV. ["Breaking news: the third possible victim of the down city murder has been found. The 3rd possible victim of serial murder killed at the café. Like the victims before, the victim had been murdered without any weapons found on the scene. The victim had been attacked once before and was already hospitalized."] He makes call someone and asks about the death person "hello. Ms. Jessie?"

He goes to police station and collects before 2 death cases by changing his form into an officer. Then he takes seat in his car and looks in to cases, when he opens 1st file he looks in to photo of dead person, then he gets shocked and that, she was the person who met him at the beginning in the bar, later he opens second file she looks like a girl who was his partner in his history writing project.

He meets hansika, "all these women were involved with you?" "Why does this case make you troubled?" "I still have good hunches. It obviously doesn't look like something a human would do, just as you noticed. It couldn't be that old man, could it? I know he has a strange state, but he can't be this wicked." "Why did the attack go after these women instead of me?" "I do know one thing for sure. If this attacker is after the women around you, think about who'll be next."

On the other hand lily was waiting for peter, that she was watched by unknown creature, there comes peter to her with tense mind "sir, you here." He looks around and worried. "What's wrong?" "Miss Lilly, I think I might be making another mistake and I may end up regretting this moment. But stay by my side." Then take a ride in his car, "sir, did something happen? "What?" "You haven't said anything for a while, and you don't look too well. I also don't understand what you meant by what you said back there." He acts like smiling and says, "Right. It didn't mean anything. You don't have to mind it." "Oh, okay." When they reach to their rooms Lilly thinks "he definitely tastes the weird things from time to time." Then a fox was watching her through the window and moves to other side, where peter senses something fishy and walks towards window, when fox was walking it turns in to a human, when peter comes out to spot it gets disappeared suddenly.

Next day morning, "sir, I'm going to college." "I'll go with you." "What?" "I'll give you a ride." "Will you?" they take a ride to collage. "Sir, why are you suddenly giving me a ride?" "I'll take you and bring you back from school for a while." "For a while? Why?" "My project has taken off, so I have to be at work at the publisher for a while." "I see." "Your collage is on the way, so I thought it'd be great to communicate together." "Of course, its great news for me." He looks at her with some curiosity that why it was great news for her. "I mean, it's great for the environment. Since we won't waste more fuels and I get to save my bus charges." He smiles for her innocence. "I'll treat you with ice cream of these days with the bus charges I saved."

He meets hansika later, "what? You're going to keep her by your side? Are you serious? Keeping her with you is honestly the most dangerous move; you said the victims were all involved with you." "I thought she'd be safer with me until I find out exactly what's going on. If anything happens to her, I'm also the one who could protect her best." "But here is the thing I don't get, if you think about it, that kid at your house was closer to you than any other women. How did she manage to stay safe?" "That's what I find relieving and questionable at the same time. Anyway, keep an eye on Miss Lilly. I ask of you." "I can't believe you're asking me for something of a favor?" "I still trust this hunch you still have left." "You trust me? Well, I'll see you; I'll keep my eyes on her if I have any extra time." "Okay."

When Lilly and swetha are walking in the campus, hansika follows her like a bodyguard, then Lilly and swetha fells uncomfortable, "hay, hansika. The road is very big. Why are you walking right behind me?" "I must have been gum in my past life." Even she stares her in class by sitting by her side, "hansika, why are you keeping staring at me?" swetha makes a punching word, "tell me about it. Were you a CCTV in your past life?" she gives no response. From her back someone was staring Lilly, and swetha senses something fishy and turns around, all of a sudden running time gets stopped and something drags Lilly to other side of hansika, as she dares to save her and she catches Lilly with her marble which is blue mad her human, then it gets disappeared by leaving Lilly and again everything gets normal. Hansika calls peter informs everything happened in the collage. Peter was so worried about the situation. Then, professor says, "We have no time, so I'll skip the attendance and go right into the lecture. Next week is waiting for you, you remember what's coming up, right?" all students shout up "yes." But Lilly and hansika were confused about next week, and then hansika speaks up, “what about next week? What is it?” then Lilly remembers something and gets scared and calls peter, “sir, what am I going to do? I’m scared.” Peter gets suspicious “what’s going on Miss Lilly?” “I’m about to take my midterms.” He gets relaxed by it, “oh, and that’s scary?” “Of course, nothing is scarier than tests for college students. So I’m going to library before I go home today. You don’t have to pick me up today. ‘”oh, okay.”

Lilly finds book ‘humanity’ and speaks to herself, “right, he said he writes humanities books. Then she finds a book which was written by peter, “his book is really here.” She turns back and suddenly bumps in to a person, then her books fells down; he picks up the book and says, “You must like this book.” “Yes, thank you.” He stares at her and says, “Be careful.” Then she gets confused and stares him suddenly peter calls her in library, “Miss Lilly.” “Hay, sir.” “What are you doing?” by showing at her back, “I bumped into this man...” but he gets disappeared. “What? Where did he go?” by searching him, “he was here just now.” “Anyway, what brings you here, sir?” “I just came to browse some books.” Then she hides book which was written by him, he laughs by her hiding, “what are those? “These are related to my studies.” “I see” from far away someone watches them.

They take a ride to home, “hay, Miss Lilly. About that man you ran into at the library. What was he like? could you tell me what he was wearing, how old he looked, and anything else you remember?” “I’m not sure. It happened so quickly, so I don’t exactly remember. He seemed pretty cold, and it looked like he was in his early 30s, kind of like you. What is it?” “I was worried.” Then Lilly thinks, “What’s going on? If he’s worried that a stranger came up and talked to me...” “There are lots of awful crimes these days.” “Right, crimes. You’re right.” “So while we’re at it, I think it might be better if you avoid strangers from now on.” “Sure.” “If anything happens and seems out of the ordinary, please let me know. I get worried.” “You get worried?’ she smiles and says, “Come on, sir. I’m not a kid.” Then they reach home.

Lilly comes out from her room by hiding something at her back and calls peter where he was passing by, by showing book which was written by him, “sir, ta-da. I bought this.” He gets surprised, “why did you buy this?” “I wanted to have a read. May I get your autograph?” “I have never done that before. It’s a bit awkward.” “Oh! I see.” Peter looks her that she was disappointed and goes to dining table with the book and eats chocolate like a rat by looking him. He falls for her innocence and childishness and gives a smile with little shy, then he takes the book and gives her an autograph. She was very happy and takes book from him and looks in to it, and then she finds a funny drawing on her, “wait, is this me? That looks worse than I actually do.” “Then let me get you a new book.” “No. I’ll just keep it. You took the time to draw it.” Then she moves to her room by dancing, after she reaches near to her door, she looks in to peter, she waves her hand and dance with 2 steps and gives him a flying kiss, “good night, bye.” She goes to the room. Peter was surprised for her action of saying goodnight and laughs at it. When she enters the room she gets a message from swetha, [swetha: here’s the question and the summary on the history of late harihara and bukka.] “Then she runs into peter, “sir. May I make use of you?” he gets shocked, “what? Make use of me?” “Swetha pointed out a possible test subject for me, discussing the background for annotations of ‘Vijayanagara Empire. I want to get a detailed explanation from you, who lived through that time.” He sighs of and says, “Annotations of ‘Vijayanagara Empire. I have related products downstairs. Do you want to come with me?” she was so excited and steps on his leg, “sure.” Then he looks at her with shocking mind and laughs.

They both enters in to the basement, peter stars his lecture, and “The Vijayanagar Empire become mounted via Harihar and Bukka in 1336 advert. Once they installation this principality, Muhammad bin Tughlaq became the Sultan in Delhi. The Vijayanagar duration is split into 4 extraordinary dynasties- Sangama, Saluva, Tuluva and Aravidu. She takes a statue which belongs to Vijayanagar Empire. “And that’s called a bronze sculpture.” “It’s like table of contents in annotation. I’m highly interested in the Buddhist culture.” She looks in to the statue for a while and suddenly comes up with a words, “sir, let’s go on a trip to a famous temple after my midterm.” “A trip?” “Why not? Dot you like going on trips?” “No, it’s not that I hate it. It’s my 1st time.” “You always say it’s your 1st time, your first time living with someone, your first time having a family and your 1st time signing an autograph. You always say that. Did you only cultivate your morals over 1000 years? What would you have done without me?” he smiles while she saying all things. “I wonder.” “Then we have no choice but to go on a trip. I mean, I’ve been worried about you lately. You kept saying all these mysterious things.so I wondered if you’d adapt well once you become a human, but I think it might be your lack of experience. Since you can enlarge your experience through this chance, I'd like to go with you." "Okay, let's go on a trip." "Really?" he nodes his head, "then promise me." "I promise." he smiles to her, by seeing his smile her heart gets flutter. "It's hot here. Sir, may I borrow this book?" then she runs out from the basement.

When she was about study once she browse about temples with nice atmosphere, and she opens the books which she took from the basement there she a drawing and there was written as 'pari'. She comes out from her room with the book and goes to peter, "sir, who is pari?" he stands still, "I found this picture in the book, so I ended up seeing it. If you missed her even in your dreams, I thought she could be your first love." "Why was that in there?" "she was, wasn't she? Her photo and name, she's obviously your first love. Right?" "I guess that might be the most appropriate expression, first love." Then she gets disappointed on his words and drops the book that it fells on his feet and he feels some pain. "Miss Lilly." "Goodness, I'm sorry." She picks up the book, "thanks for showing your 1st love. I mean your book. She gives book to him and slowing goes to her room with crying face, and takes a seat on her study chair, "girl and a picture, he had lots of romantic experiences, didn't he?" she gets disappointed. "But, he drew her so gorgeously with every stroke of his brush, but he draws me like this at his autograph.

At morning they take a walk, "excuse me sir, I'm asking you without any intentions, so this question is purely academic." Then she suddenly spots that girl who was in the picture and gets shocked she was watering for flowers, "she looks like her." "What?" "No, never mind. Nothing." Then she leaves the place with disappointed face.

At cafeteria Lilly, swetha and jinn takes seat and jinn was eating with awful noise then swetha says, "Hay, you stop making that noise? You're making me lose focus." Where she was studying. "There she is. The highly sensitive swetha, who shows up during the exam period." "My sensitivity and fierceness are what made me the top student in our major. I'm going out for two more cups or instant coffee to wake up" then she lefts the place, where jinn says, "Goodness, she always overreacts." Then suddenly Lilly speaks up "hay." "Fine. I'll eat quietly." "No, it's not that. What does first love mean to men?" "First love? All of a sudden?" "I just got curious." "First love. Those two words make you feel so sentimental and painful. I had my first love back in middle school. We broke up over the most heartrending reason. She was terminally ill." "Really?" "No, she lied to me. It turns out she two-timed me with a close-friend, even though she made up such an absurd lie, I still couldn't forget her just because she was my first love, people say, all men have one room in their hearts they keep for life. The room where they keep their first love until the day they die." "So if he doesn't die, she lives on it that room of life?" "Exactly. She checks in, but there is no check-out hour. You may face a peak season with other people you love, but that room is always sold out. No one can take it." He was emotional and shouts by that words, and Lilly was angry and beats him up and gets disappoint.

When Lilly was coming out of collage peter calls her, "hello, sir." "What time will you be done today?" "Well, I don't think you have to pick me up today. No, nothing is going on. I just wanted to walk a little." Then she finds peter outside waiting for her. Then he comes near to her, "then lets walk together." They take a walk, "so why did you suddenly want to walk today?" "Just because. Weather was so nice." Then they go through the place where pari spots before, Lilly looks at her and stops far away, "Miss Lilly?" when he was about look pari she distracts him, "let's go. I said I'll buy you ice-cream with the bus charge I saved. Let's go eat that now." They take a seat in ice-cream parlor. Then Lilly won't eat anything and sits calmly and disappointed. "Is something wrong, Miss Lilly?" "What?" "You don't seem very well." "No, it's nothing." She thinks a while and asks, "Anyway, jinn told me that all men have a room in their hearts and in that room, they keep their first love for life. Is that true?" "I'm not sure." "What about you?" "She suddenly came back to me for a very long time." Then she speaks for herself, "I feel like such a fool."

Next day she takes place at classroom alone and speaks herself, "I hate myself for getting concerned over something that happened hundreds of years ago" later jinn come to class and spots her, "what's going on? Why are you sighing? Is that guy you asked out troubling you again?" "What?" "I knew something was up when you suddenly asked me about men's first love. Did his first love show up?" "No, that's not the case." "Then just forget it. You don't have to mind the past, it's not like you can undo what already happened." "I know that. But I get jealous. I hate how ridiculous I am, but that's how I feel. What's wrong with me?" "I think that's only natural. There comes a moment in everyone's life when they lose their usual speed, it happens once you like someone."

When Lilly was roaming in collage Sameer meets up, but she ignores him and about to leave, Sameer comes on her way, "hay. How are your studies going for the midterms? Do you start tomorrow?" "Why do you care?" "Well, I wanted to bid you good luck and I quit smoking. You said you hated it." Suddenly hansika shows up there, "Lilly, let's eat lunch." "What? With me?" "Is there another Lilly here? Let's go." Hansika says by looking to Sameer, "Sameer, what you need to quit is your interest is Lilly, not smoking." They leaves place to cafeteria and they will be taking lunch. "Why have you been like this to me lately?" "Like what?" "I mean, you're always around me and you suddenly wanted to eat." Then hansika slips her tongue and says, "Because I was asked to." And she suddenly stops saying. "You were asked to do this?" "This monk I know asked me to be kind to others. That's how I can gain virtue and end up in paradise." "I see. So you were a Buddhist." "Something like that. But I don't even expect to end up in paradise. I just want to live according to my fate and place enjoying this troublesome life to the fullest. That's all I want." Lilly laughs for her words. "Hansika, you sometimes seem like you have years of experience from the way you talk." "Why are you criticizing me while I'm being kind to you?" "Criticizing you? It's a good thing to come off as an experienced person." "I'm not sure. I hate it when people say, I seem seasoned as if I have years of experience. I looked like humans think longevity is a blessing and want to live forever. Imagine if you live for almost an eternity, how do you think it'll feel?" Lilly was confused for her words. Then they completes lunch, when Lilly was walking alone in the campus, a person was watching her from rooftop of the building. Then he senses something behind her and says, "I didn't expect you to find me." Then he finds hansika who found him. "It has been a while, fox." "Don't call me a fox. I'm a human now." "Then live like a human. Stop coming to place like this by using his petty magic." She was afraid, about the words, "don't be afraid, I don't mean that I'll ruin your life right now." Then she gets relaxed. "Old man, you know about this, right?" "Know what?" "The mysterious happenings surrounding peter." Then he smiles. "I can tell by your face that you do know. Help him." "I'm not sure. Don't you think this is his job?" suddenly peter appears and says, "If you have anything to say, you can tell me." "Peter, what have you been doing to this day? Hansika is younger than you, yet she became a human ages ago." "I said I wanted to become a human. Then you told me to collect human energy to become one. I've always known you weren't the kindest guy since then, it must have been lots of fun, if you just stood back and watched me to this day." "Fun? I may not look like it, but I'm a mountain god. What benefits would I get from troubling you in repeated times? My job is to take care of your destiny which is why I have been watching over her." Then hansika speak up. "Are you saying you're the reason she has been safe?" "Of course. She's been protected by my magic spell. I was looking around her at times and around you at others." Peter speaks out, "so, from whom have you been protecting us?" "When a fox lives 1000 years, it turns into a beast. I didn't want you to turn into such a wicked creature. That's the thing, I thought I might as well eliminate you, if you fail to become a human within 1000 years." Hansika covers him and says, "Why would you suddenly talk about elimination?" "There appeared one who goes against nature and disrupts the order. A beast that have lived a thousand years and failed to become a human refused to be eliminated and turned in to an evil spirit and it yearns to possess your marble." Then hansika speaks out, 'wait, an evil spirit yearns to possess the marble? What does it need it for?" "It has a silly belief that it might make it a human. "You should have made sure to eliminate it in the first place. You had one job. So where the evil spirit is called beast or whatever?' "Even if you don't try, you'll eventually bump into it. I couldn't find what it wanted, and it will now try to find it from you, the owner of the marble. And now a human's life is in my hand because I did my job. I do not want to disturb order; I think I should stop here. I saying I'm not protecting her anymore." Then peter was about to talk, "what does that..." "Without listening to him he gets disappeared. He was more worried about Lilly.

Where Lilly was passing by the place when she was seen pari and she spots pari and stares at her, all of a sudden pari looks in to her then smiles cunningly, then peter shows up on Lilly, "Miss Lilly." "Sir." "Are you okay?" "What do you mean?" "Why didn't you call me? I said I would come pick you up." "Right. The class suddenly got canceled, so..." then he finds pari and gets shocked, slowly Lilly grabs his hand and says, "sir, let's go home now." "I want you to go first. I'll catch up with you right away." She gets disappointed and moves from there, later peter reaches to pari and says. "I know why you appeared with that face. You want the marble." She cunningly looks into him and turns in to terrible appearance and says 'you don't have the marble anyway." He tries to attack it but it gets disappeared.

She was studying at home, while she was studying she thinks about the flower shop pari and peter, then she hears a sound, then she comes out from her room and looks at peter room, she finds nothing there and about to go to her room, then all lights gets blink from a second and Lilly feels something wired and looks back, she finds peter, where he was looking around and worried, "sir. Is everything okay? Did something happen at the flower shop?" then she hesitates and says, "Never mind." Then she turns around and about to leave, then peter grabs her hand and says, "Miss Lilly, all I think about are you, I promise I would protect you, and I always think about how I can keep my word. I meant everything I said to you. So... trust me." Then they live to their respective rooms.

She sits in her study chair and thinks, "It's funny, and how a few words can make me feel better, though I have been upset the whole time." Then peter knocks the door, "yes, sir." Then he comes to her room "Miss Lilly." "What's up?" "Well... I don't feel comfortable leaving you alone. Would mind staying with me tonight? She gets shock for the words. They both have sleep in living room that Lilly sleep on sofa and peter sleep on the floor.

Lilly, swetha and jinn comes down trough downstairs from the exam hall. Then jinn says to swetha, "seriously, everything you mentioned was on the exam." Then all the three takes seat besides the table and Lilly was disappointed and says "what am I going to do? I messed up my first exam." Then she suddenly thinks off, "I shouldn't have stayed with him for two days. I couldn't focus." "Jinn speaks up, "I almost got a heart attack when I got the exam paper. All the exam materials swetha shared with me were on the exam. I had so much to write, but there wasn't much space for it." Then Lilly gets surprised and says, "What? Am I the only one who messed it up?" jinn say, "Yes. You're the only one. You'll let me see your notes and the exam materials again, right?" "Where is your teasing?" "No, no, I'll be nice to you. From next on." "Not interested. I've got to go." She leaves the place where jinn speak up, "she said she's studying in the library the whole night. Let's go join her." "You are right, but..." "The exam is tomorrow morning. You don't want to waste time travelling back and forth. Hay, do you want to take the same class again next semester?" "No. Let's go."

On the Lilly calls peter and say," I'm sorry. I can't go home today. I really messed up the exam. I think I should study with my friends today." "Okay good luck. And call me if something happens." "Okay. I'll text you immediately." Then she enters in to the library though peter stays at her side watching her behind.

She was searching for a book in the library. Peter thinks, "As the ghost changes his form then why can't he..." he gets suspicious by looking in to his face in the mirror and remembers the three girls who have killed by the ghost with his form. "When Lilly was searching book peter suddenly appears back of her. "Hi, sir. What are you doing here?" "I came to see you, I was wondering if you were doing all right." "Oh, I guess it bothered you that I'm staying out." Then he looks in to her stomach where he can find red stone, and he smiles at it and says "there you are." "what" the slowly about to touch her then all of a sudden a book fells down then Lilly looks back in the book. Then with in a fraction of second someone drags him to other side. When Lilly turns back he finds no one finds there. Then peter comes in to dark area with a ghost then there goes dreadful war between them. Then peter wins against the ghost. Then Lilly messages him. ["Lilly: sir, why did you suddenly disappear? Is everything alright."] Then he suddenly appears in front of her and says, "Everything is alright." "Gosh, you scared me. What happened? I was worried about you." He gives smiles, and then Lilly asks, "What did you mean by, 'there you are'?" "I said that because I found you." Then he pity her, he smiles and says, "Now, everything will be all right." "What do you mean?" "If you want to come home because you get tired or sleepy, call me. I'll come pick you up any time." "okay." Then they disperse, on the way peter finds hansika, they both move to a place near library, "are you okay? I guess all kinds of things happen when you live a long life. Now, don't worry about other things and focus on your original goal. You're almost there. I know it's upsetting, but there must be a reason why the marble changed its color for the first time. So do everything you can to keep her. If you become an evil spirit, just like the old man said." Then he remembers the words said by old man. "How does it feel to witness the vein end? I want you to remember this day. It can happen to you too. Think of the girl as your last hope and become a human. I truly wish you won't meet a tragic end like this." "Why aren't you saying anything?" He stands still.

From exam hall three of friends will come out and Lilly speaks out, "gosh, it's finally over. It feels so good." Jinn say, "Thanks, swetha. You helped me a lot." "If you thank me so much, buy me dinner tonight." Jinn say, "Okay. Why don't we go now? Have so much of food." Swetha was so excited and says "I'd love to! Where should we go?" "Where ever you want to." Then Lilly gets a message, ["peter: Miss Lilly, now your exams are finished, why don't we go on a trip?"] she was happy for message and she says "guys, I have an appointment. I've got to go. I'm sorry. I'll buy you dinner next time, dory. Bye." She moves in a hurry hen both of then calls her. "Lilly, Lilly." "It's okay. It's just the two of us, so it'll be cheaper, come on. Let's go." "Forget it. Let's do it another time. I mean I don't want to be hanging around the campus looking like this, you know what I mean." "Listen, my friend. I really didn't want to say this because you helped me a lot, but why do you keep calling yourself topper?" she ignores him and leaves.

Lilly hurry to peter and finds him, there peter walks near her where Lilly runs towards him and peter says, "Be careful you might fall." Within seconds she was about to fall by touching her own leg, the peter hugs her in order to save her from falling. "See? I told you to be careful." "Right, I almost fell. By the way, why a trip all of a sudden?" "We agreed to go on a trip together when your exams are finished." "Right. But I didn't know it would be on the very day the exam was over." "Should we try another day then?" "No. you say that only when you buy lottery tickets. Let's go." "Let's take a bus this time."

They take a ride in bus and having fun "why did you suggest we ride a bus this time?" "Well, I wanted to go slowly." "Slowly. That sounds great." Then Lilly was happy and smiles, peter takes his mobile and takes her pictures and takes both pictures. They reaches the place looks like forest but decorated in wonder. They both will have fun and enjoys by playing. Lilly finds a small statue on the way takes it then she makes a wish, by seeing her peter also makes a wish.

They both take a seat, and Lilly speaks up, "by the way, do you have a wish too? I mean, you can use magic whenever you want; you've been accumulating wealth for almost a thousand years, and you so tall and handsome. I wonder what you can possibly have. Oh, maybe you wished the marble comes out soon so you can be a human." "I made a wish for you." "For me?" "You have a beautiful smile, so I wished you would get to smile often. You can make your dreams come true, so I wished you wouldn't give up on what you like. And I wished you wouldn't get hurt by others. I wished you would always be well." She feels something great by his words... when it was night all area looks wonderful by the lightening. She looks around and takes a video where peter follows her at her back. "It's pretty. Don't you think, sir? I'm so glad we came here." All of a sudden she turns back to peter "sir. Let's come back here next year." She was very happy, where peter seems silent. "Actually, earlier in front of that statue, I wished I could come back here next here with you. But not like this. I wished you could come with me as a human." Then she speaks up with silence face, "Miss Lilly, do you remember what I said then?" "What do you mean?" "I said I never had a family, but I felt like I got one now. I really meant what I said. Nobody has ever stayed with me for this long. I've been used to being along. Then... I met you and you happened to become special to me." He recalls all happy moments with her. He becomes silent for a while and says "I lied. I knew how to take out the stone from the beginning. But I lied to you. I needed energy to become human, and you happened to be there." She was shocked for it and cries. He comes closer to her "you won't remember a thing. When you wake up, everything will be over." He takes her to his hands "you just had a short dream." She cries with a pain silently "as of now everything have ended." Then he takes the stone from her.

TO BE CONTINUED

9 798885 551564

Printed by Libri Plureos GmbH in Hamburg,
Germany